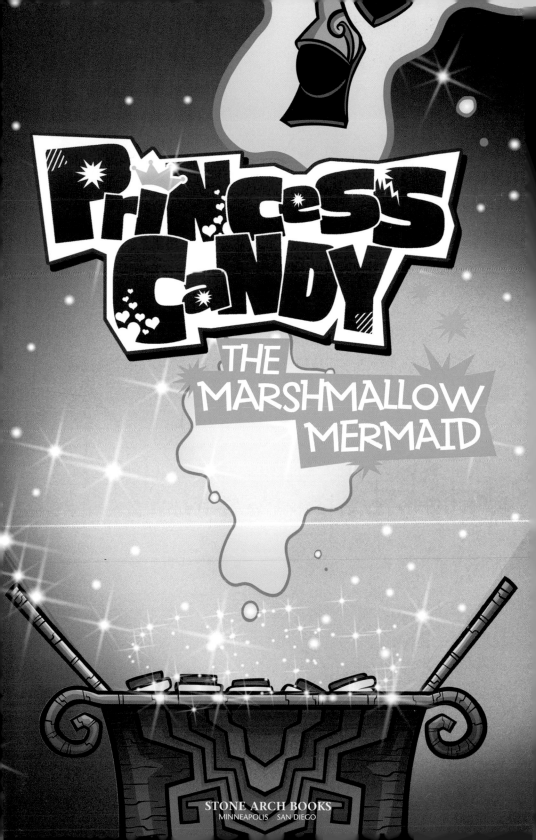

PRiNCeSS CaNDY

THE MARSHMALLOW MERMAID

STONE ARCH BOOKS
MINNEAPOLIS   SAN DIEGO

Graphic Sparks are published by Stone Arch Books,
A Capstone Imprint
151 Good Counsel Drive, P.O. Box 669
Mankato, Minnesota 56002
www.capstonepub.com

Library of Congress Cataloging-in-Publication Data

Dahl, Michael.
  The marshmallow mermaid / by Michael Dahl ; illustrated by Jeff Crowther.
     p. cm. -- (Graphic sparks. Princess Candy)
  ISBN 978-1-4342-1588-8 (lib. bdg.)
  ISBN 978-1-4342-2802-4 (pbk.)
  1. Graphic novels. [1. Graphic novels. 2. Superheroes--Fiction. 3. Mermaids--
Fiction. 4. Schools--Fiction.] I. Crowther, Jeff, ill. II. Title.
  PZ7.7.D34Mar 2010
  741.5'973--dc22
                                          2009011408

Summary: At Halo Nightly's school, the swimmers
are disappearing from the boys' swim team. No one
can figure it out, until Halo stars investigating.
A deadly mermaid lives in a cave connected
to the school swimming pool. Halo will have
to use her special candy to turn into
various underwater fauna, such as a
hammerhead shark
or an octopus, to defeat the
hungry girl-fish!

Creative Director:
Heather Kindseth

Graphic Designer:
Brann Garvey

Printed in the United States of America in Stevens Point, Wisconsin.
042011
006181R

Princess Candy

THE MARSHMALLOW MERMAID

WRITTEN BY
MICHAEL DAHL

ILLUSTRATED BY
JEFF CROWTHER

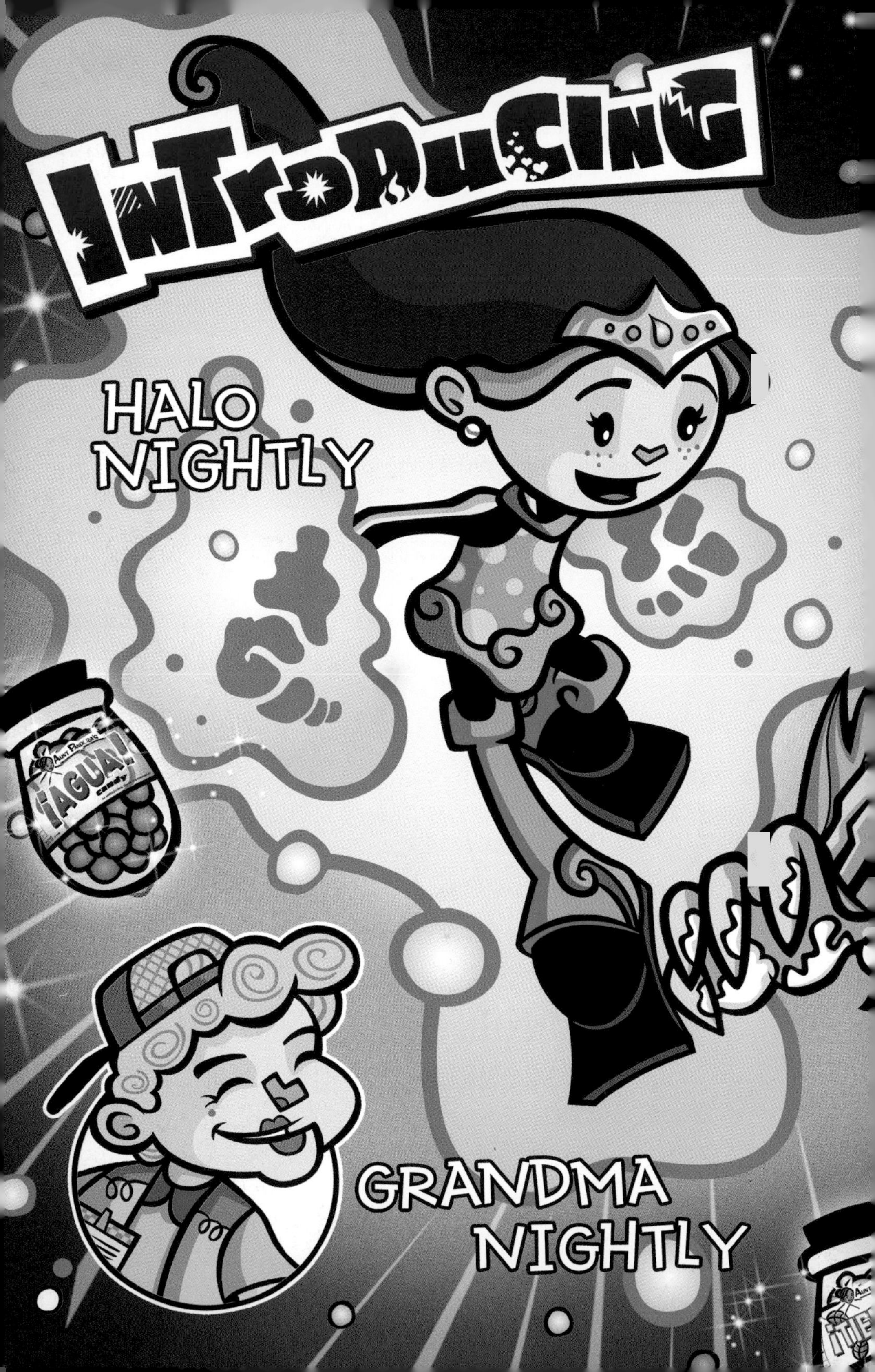
INTRODUCING
HALO NIGHTLY
¡AGUA!
GRANDMA NIGHTLY

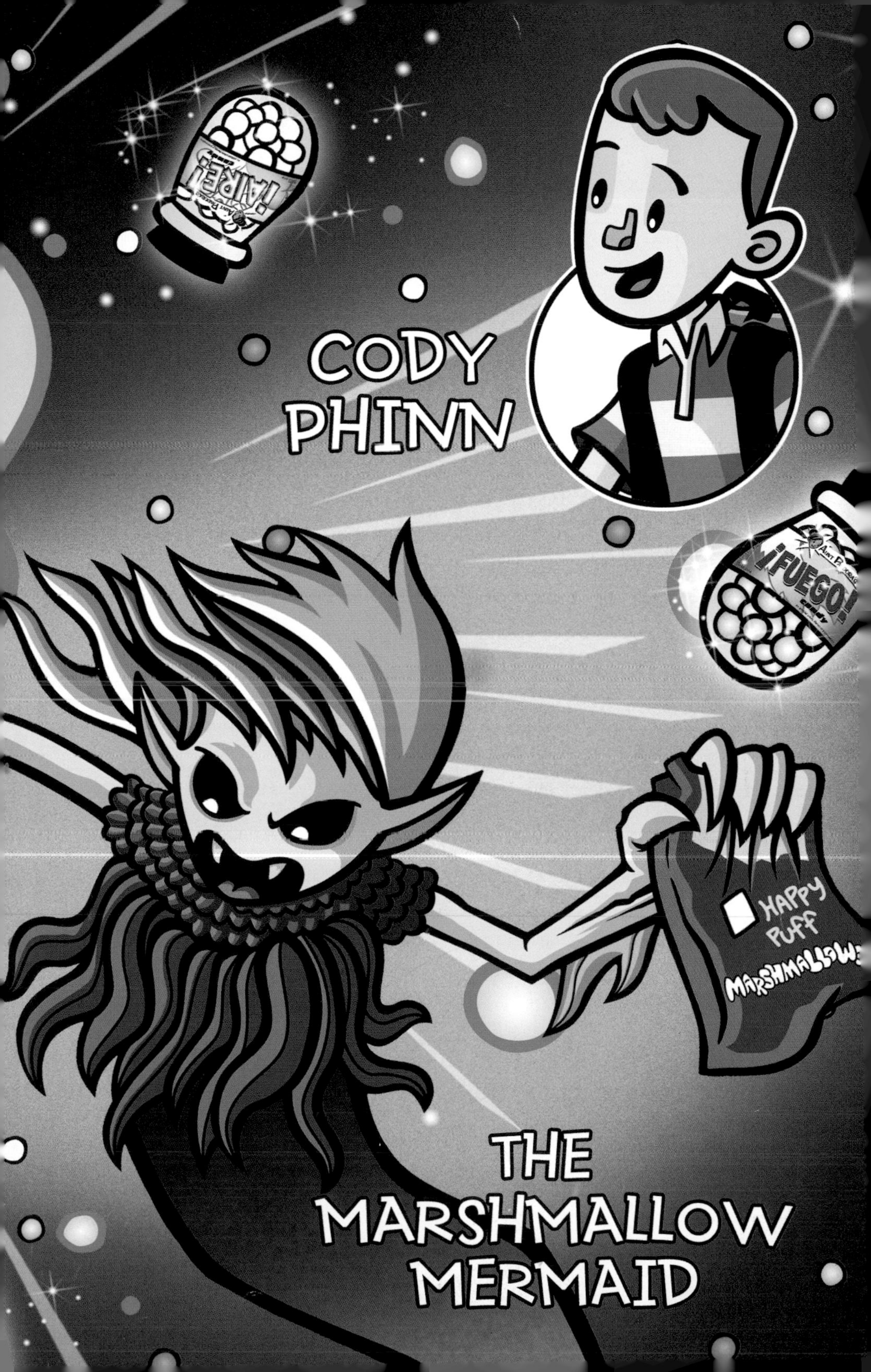

¡AIRE!
CODY PHINN
¡FUEGO!
HAPPY PUFF MARSHMALLOWS
THE MARSHMALLOW MERMAID

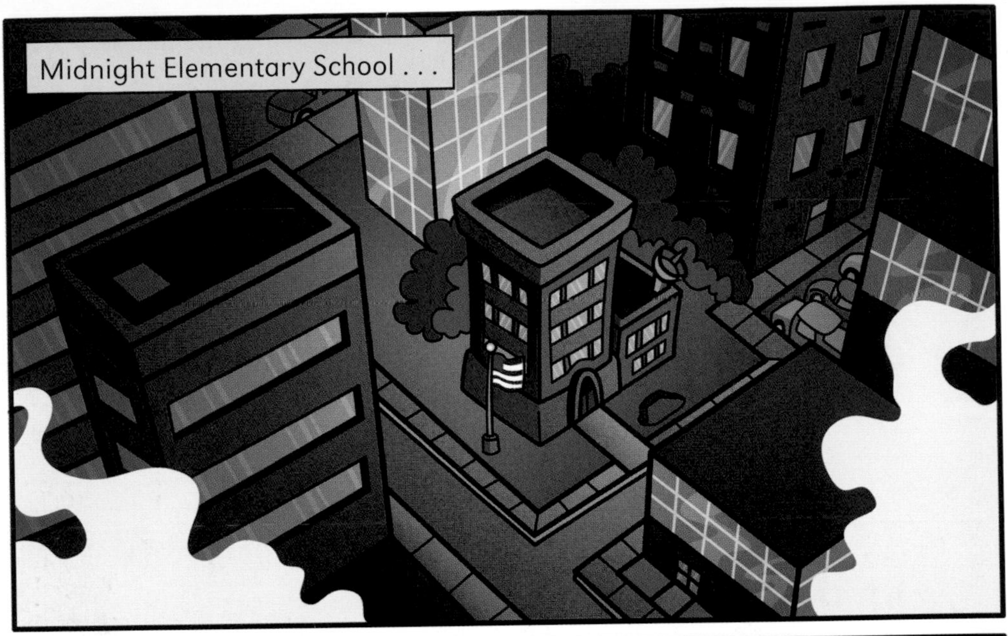
Midnight Elementary School . . .

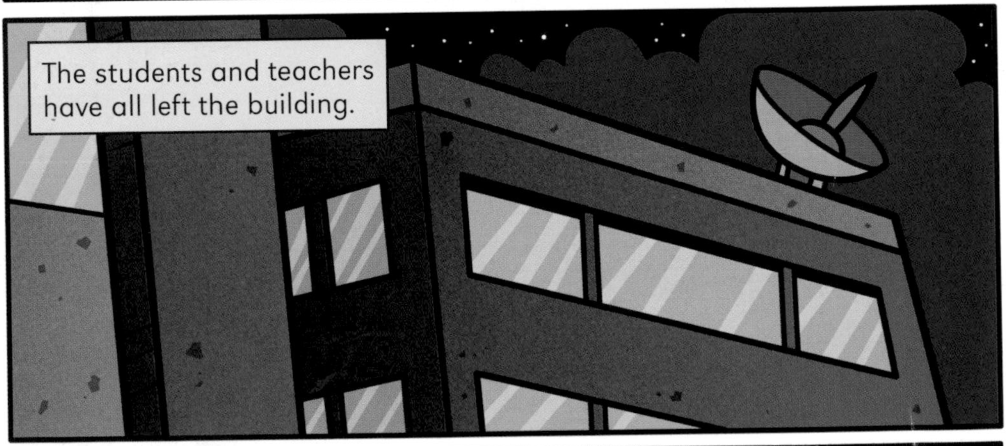
The students and teachers have all left the building.

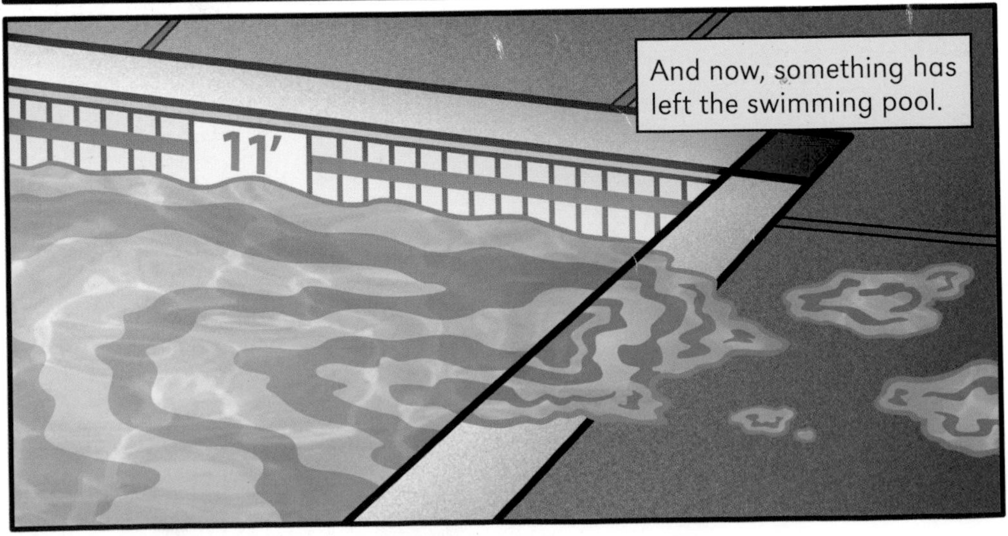
11'
And now, something has left the swimming pool.

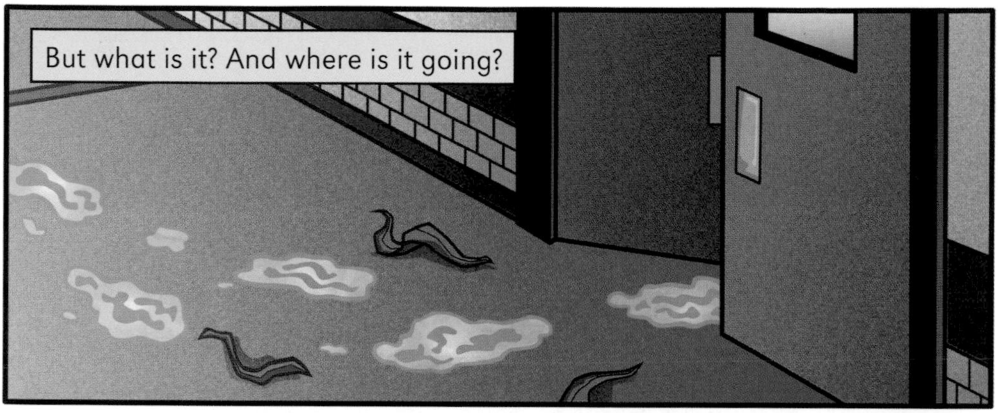
But what is it? And where is it going?

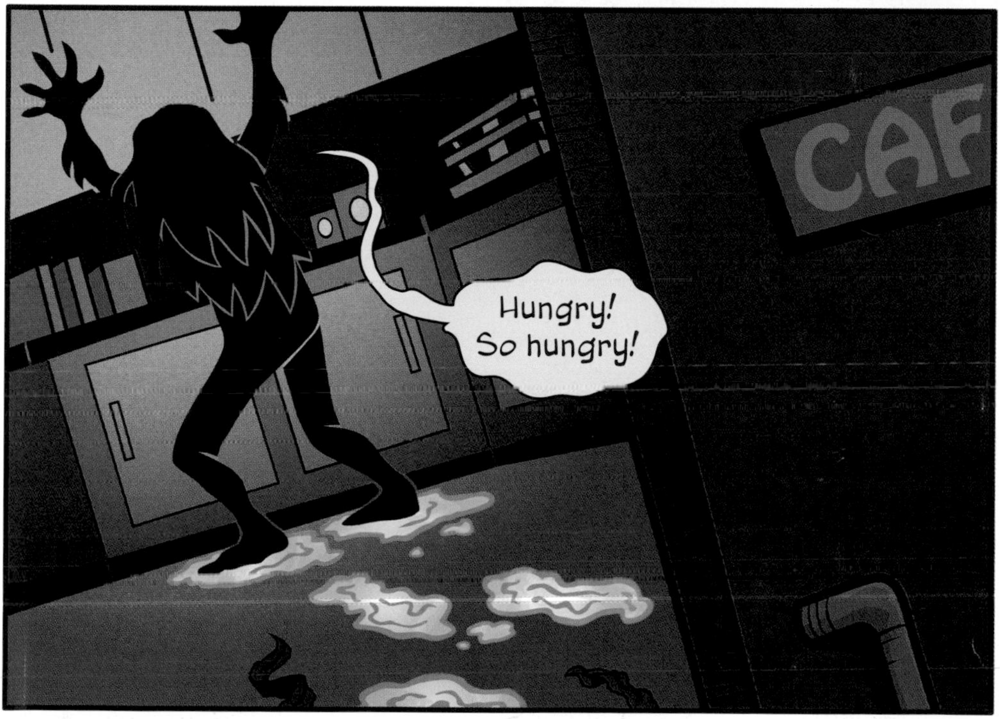
CAF
Hungry!
So hungry!

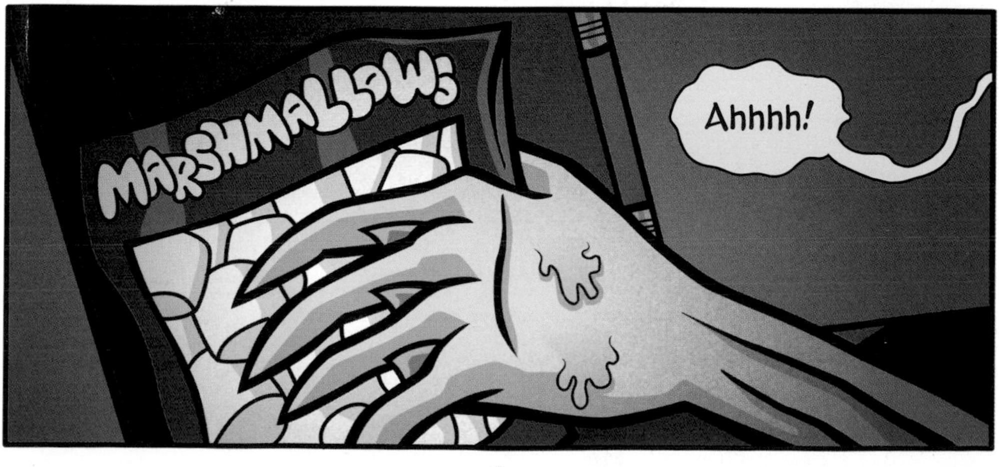
MARSHMALLOWS
Ahhhh!

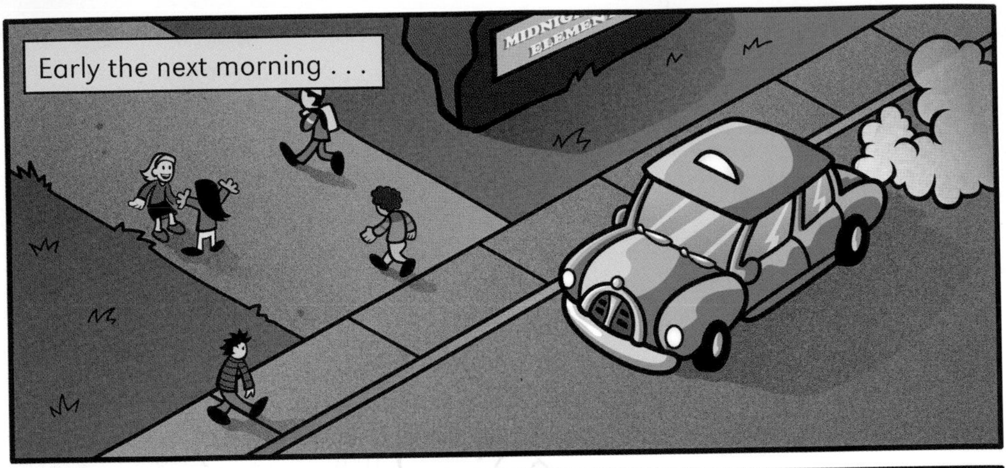
Early the next morning . . .
MIDNIGH
ELEMEN

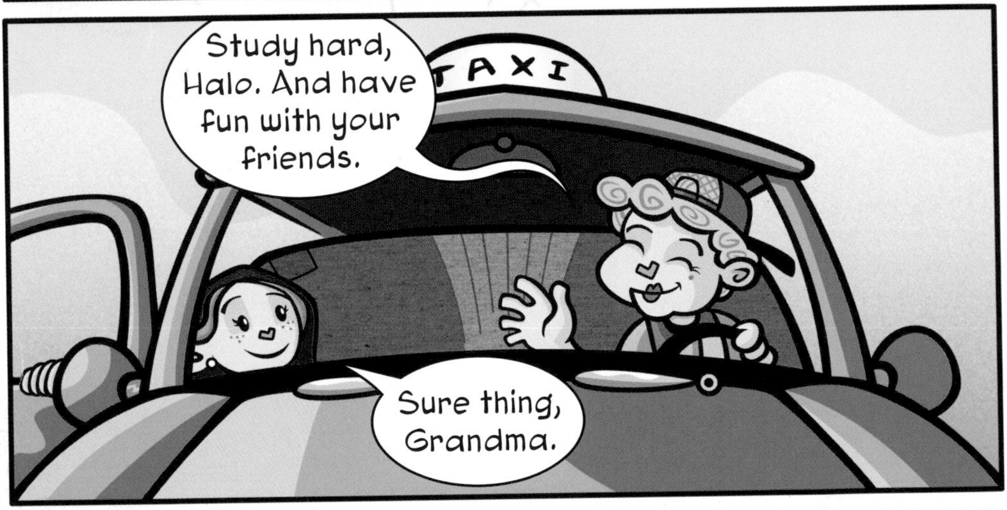
TAXI
Study hard, Halo. And have fun with your friends.
Sure thing, Grandma.

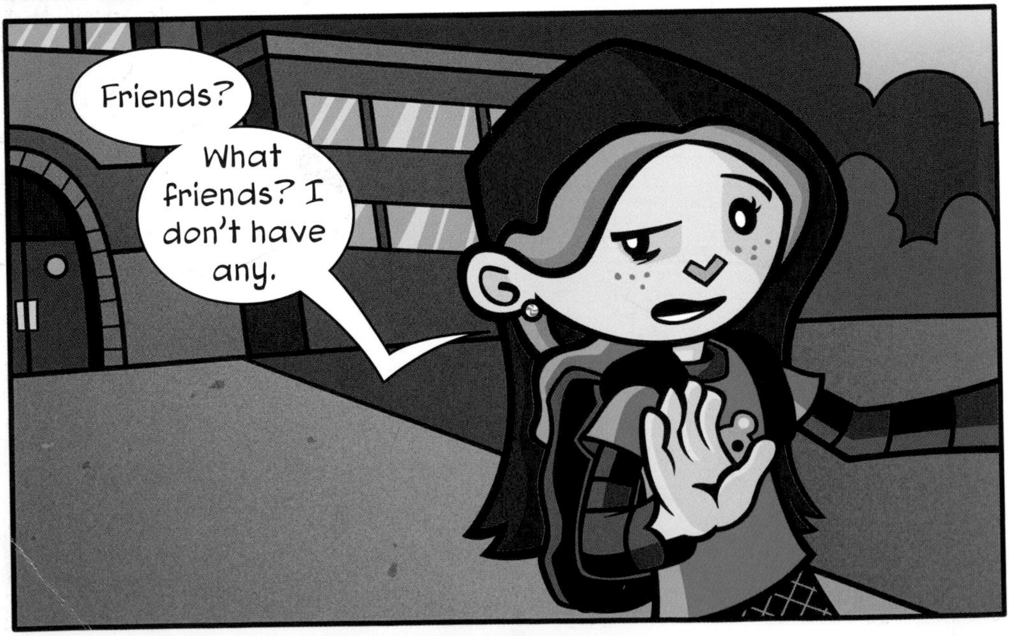
Friends?
What friends? I don't have any.

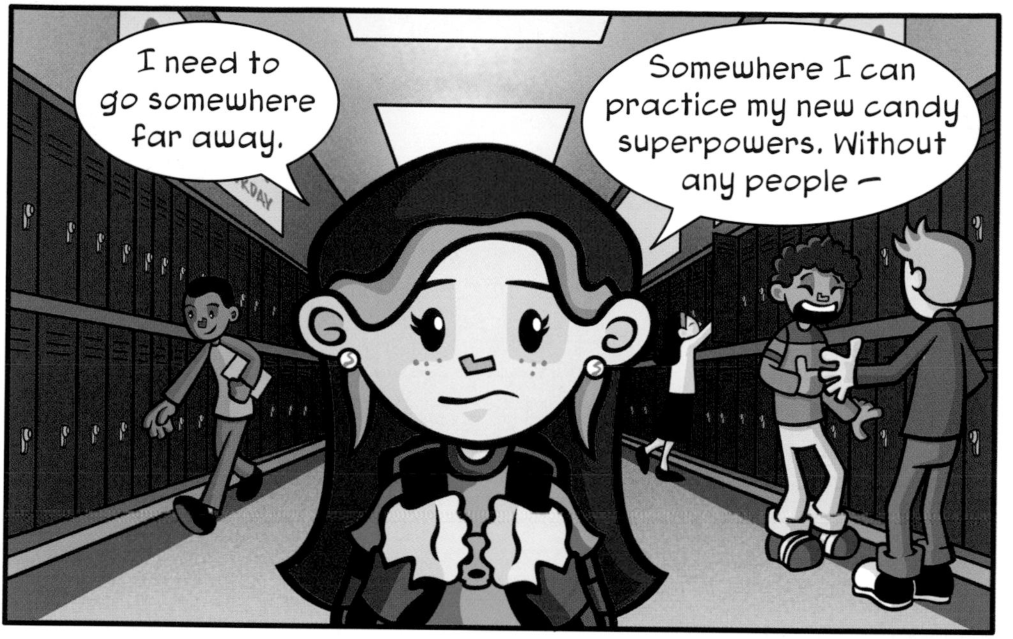
I need to go somewhere far away.
Somewhere I can practice my new candy superpowers. Without any people —

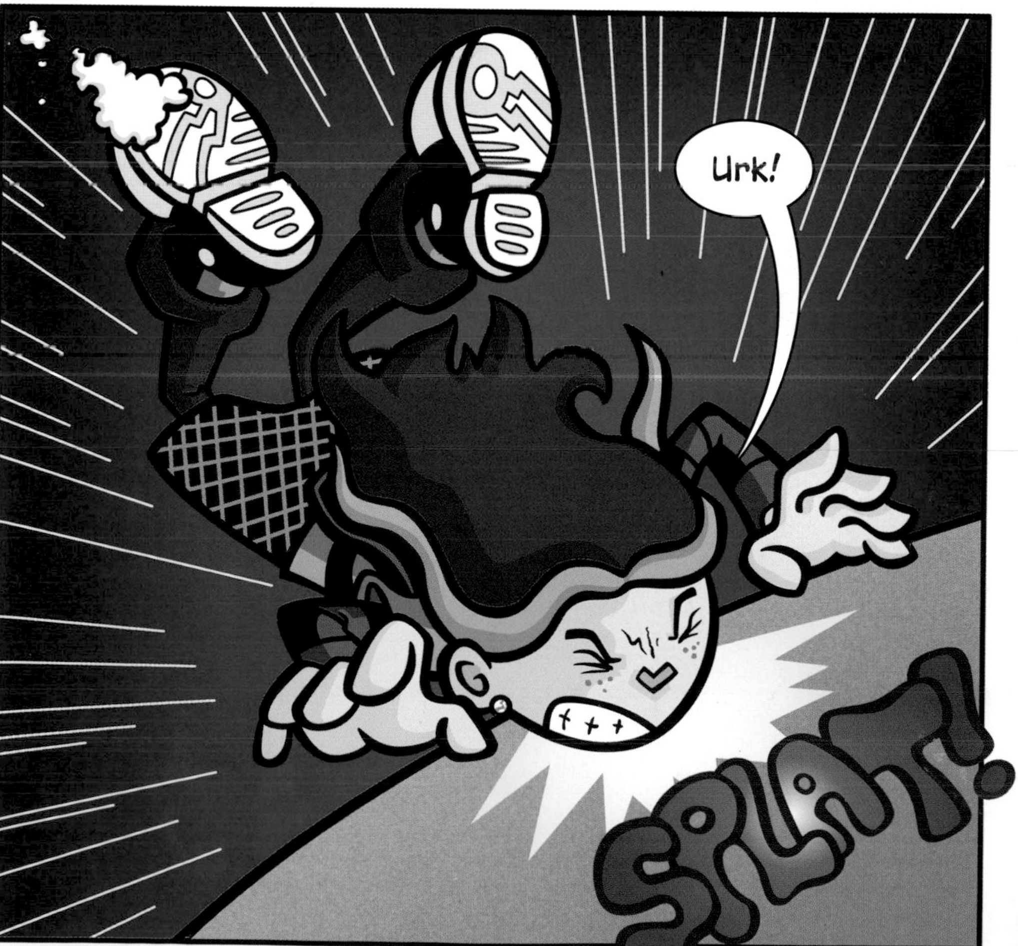
Urk!
SPLAT!

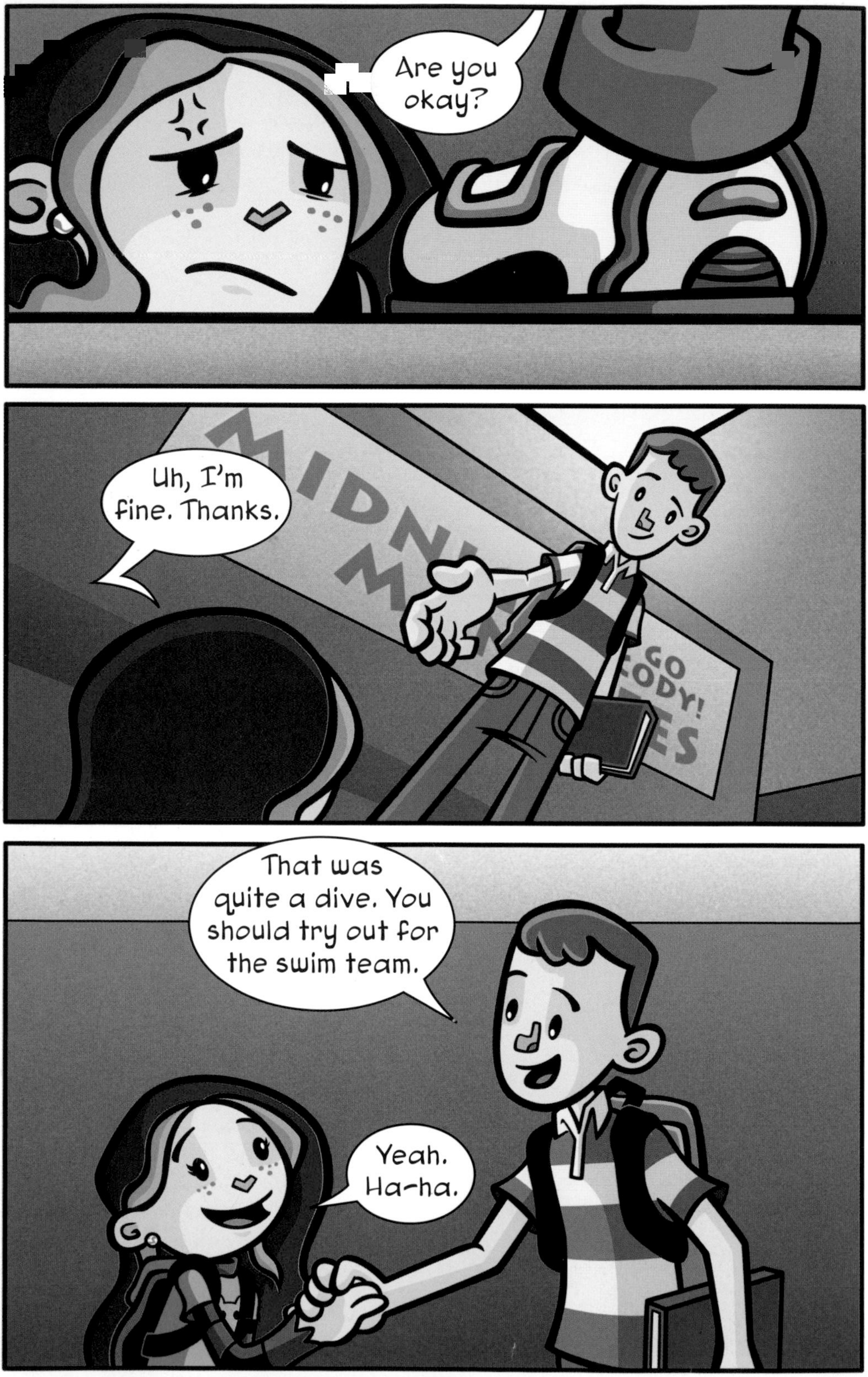
Are you okay?
Uh, I'm fine. Thanks.
That was quite a dive. You should try out for the swim team.
Yeah. Ha-ha.

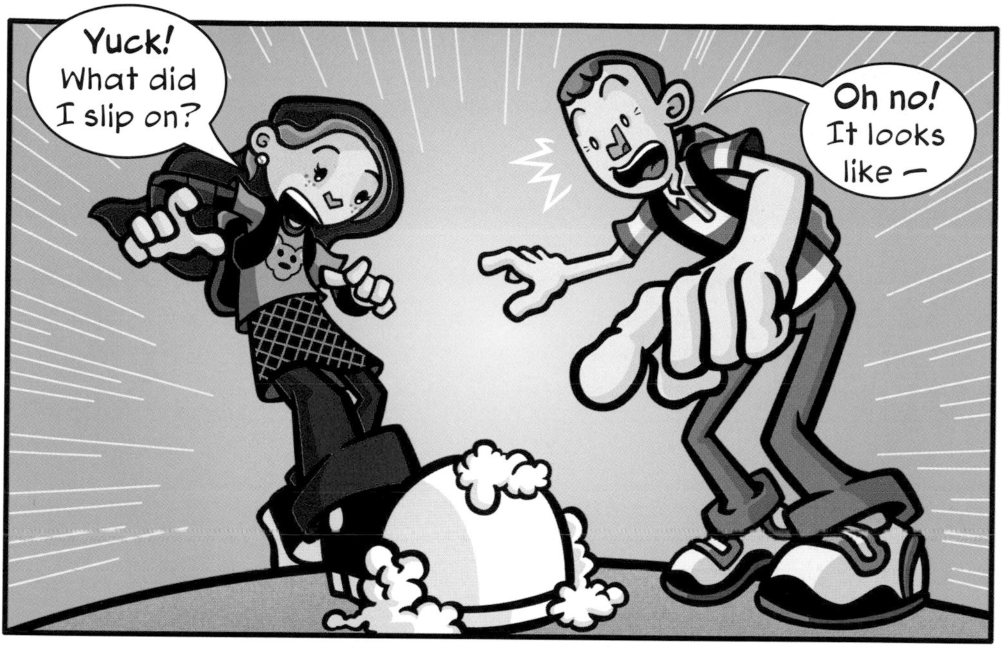
Yuck! What did I slip on?
Oh no! It looks like —

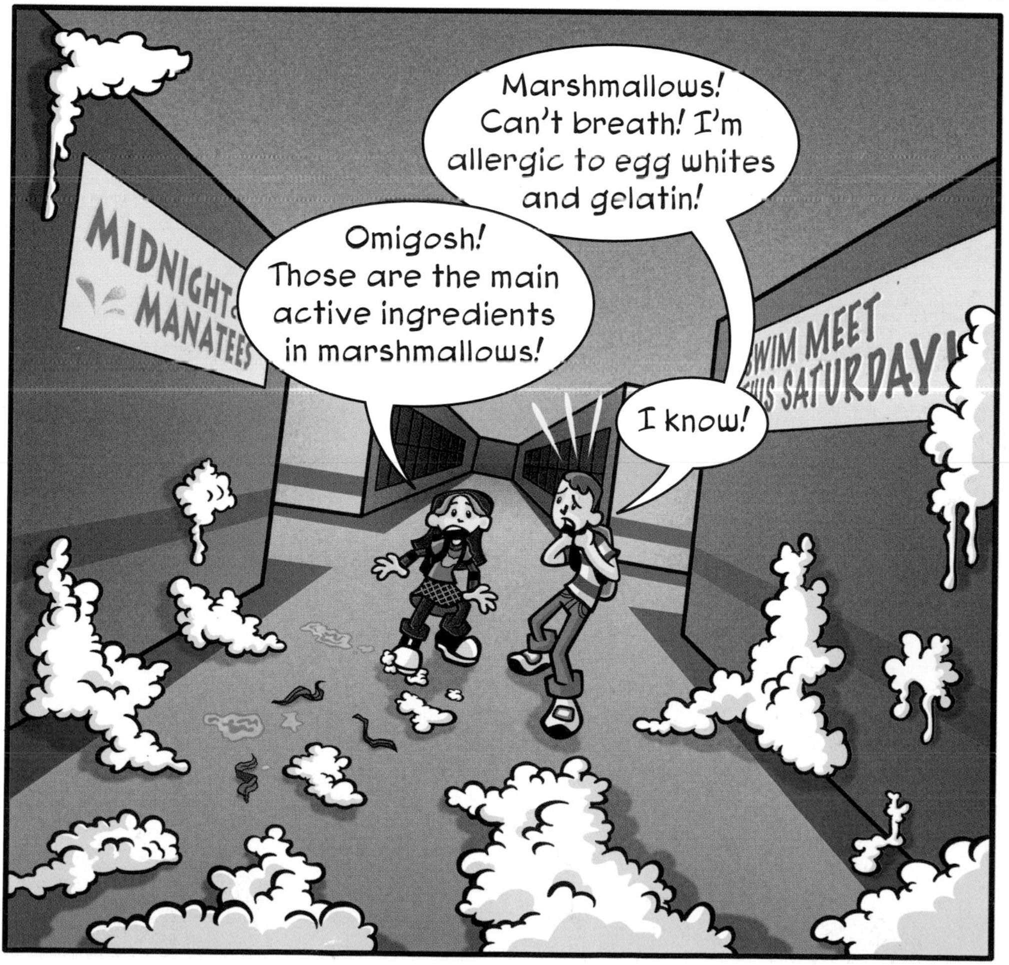
MIDNIGHT MANATEES
SWIM MEET THIS SATURDAY!
Omigosh! Those are the main active ingredients in marshmallows!
Marshmallows! Can't breath! I'm allergic to egg whites and gelatin!
I know!

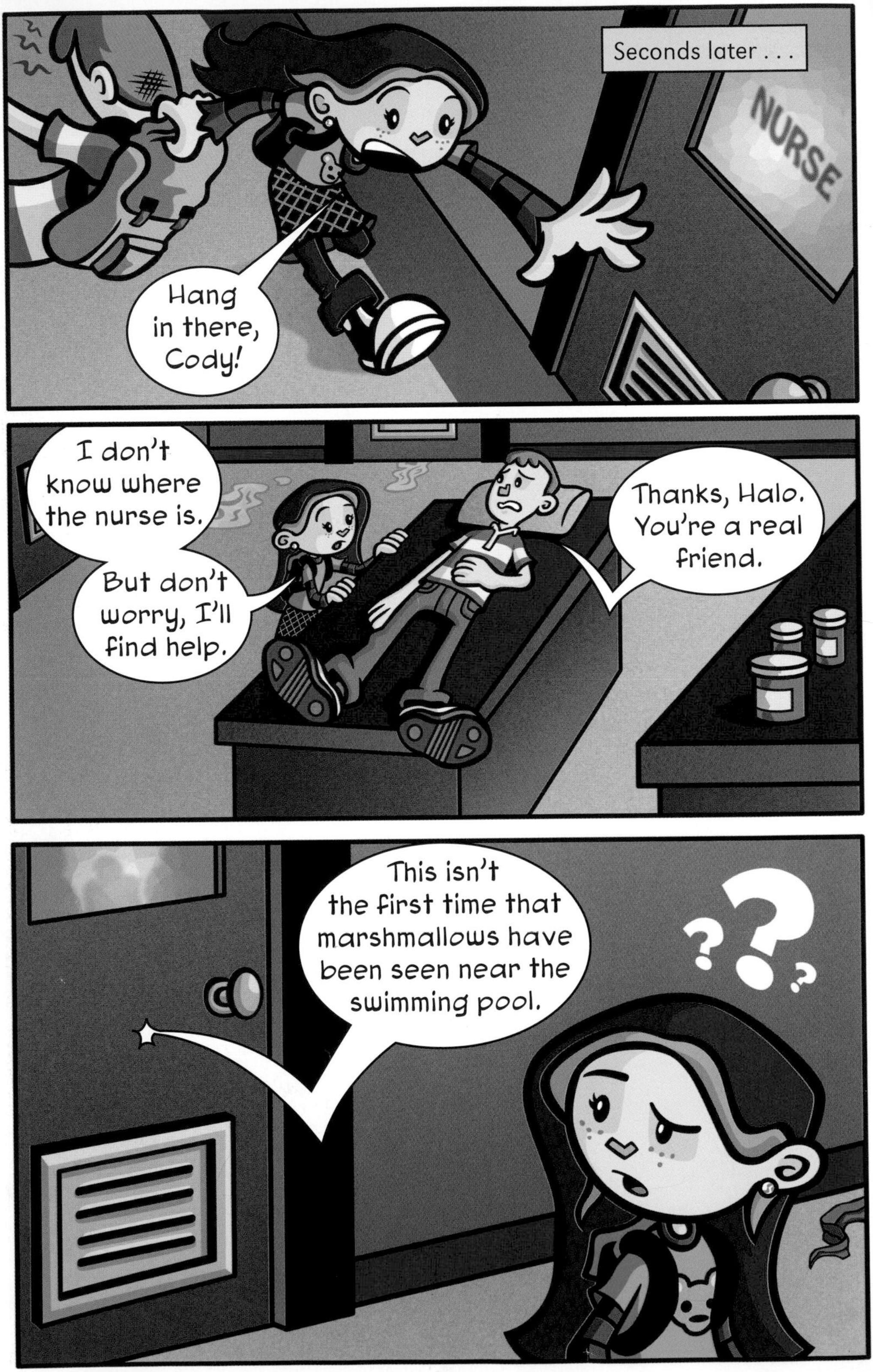
Seconds later . . .
NURSE
Hang in there, Cody!
I don't know where the nurse is.
But don't worry, I'll find help.
Thanks, Halo. You're a real friend.
This isn't the first time that marshmallows have been seen near the swimming pool.

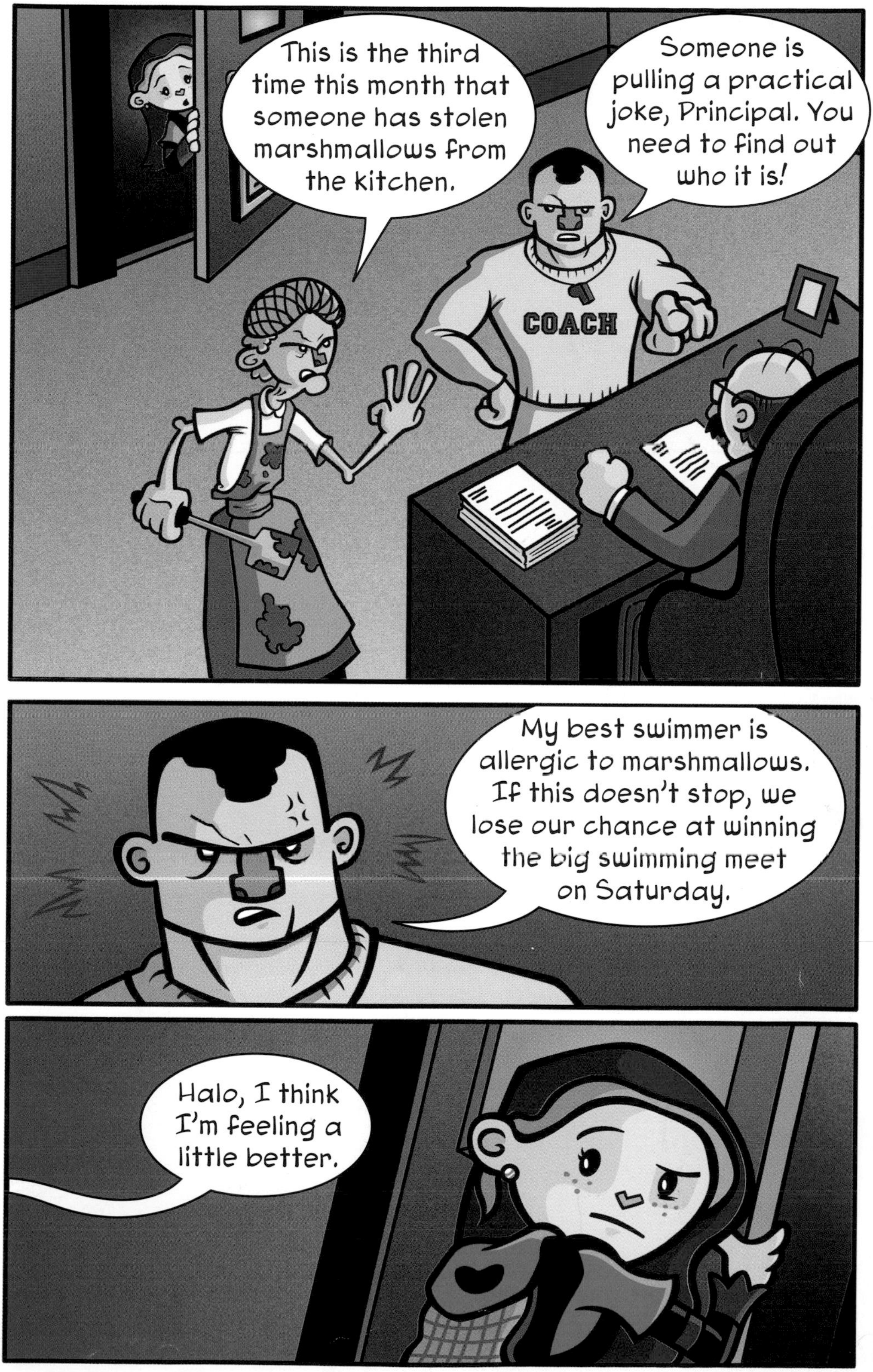
This is the third time this month that someone has stolen marshmallows from the kitchen.
Someone is pulling a practical joke, Principal. You need to find out who it is!
COACH
My best swimmer is allergic to marshmallows. If this doesn't stop, we lose our chance at winning the big swimming meet on Saturday.
Halo, I think I'm feeling a little better.

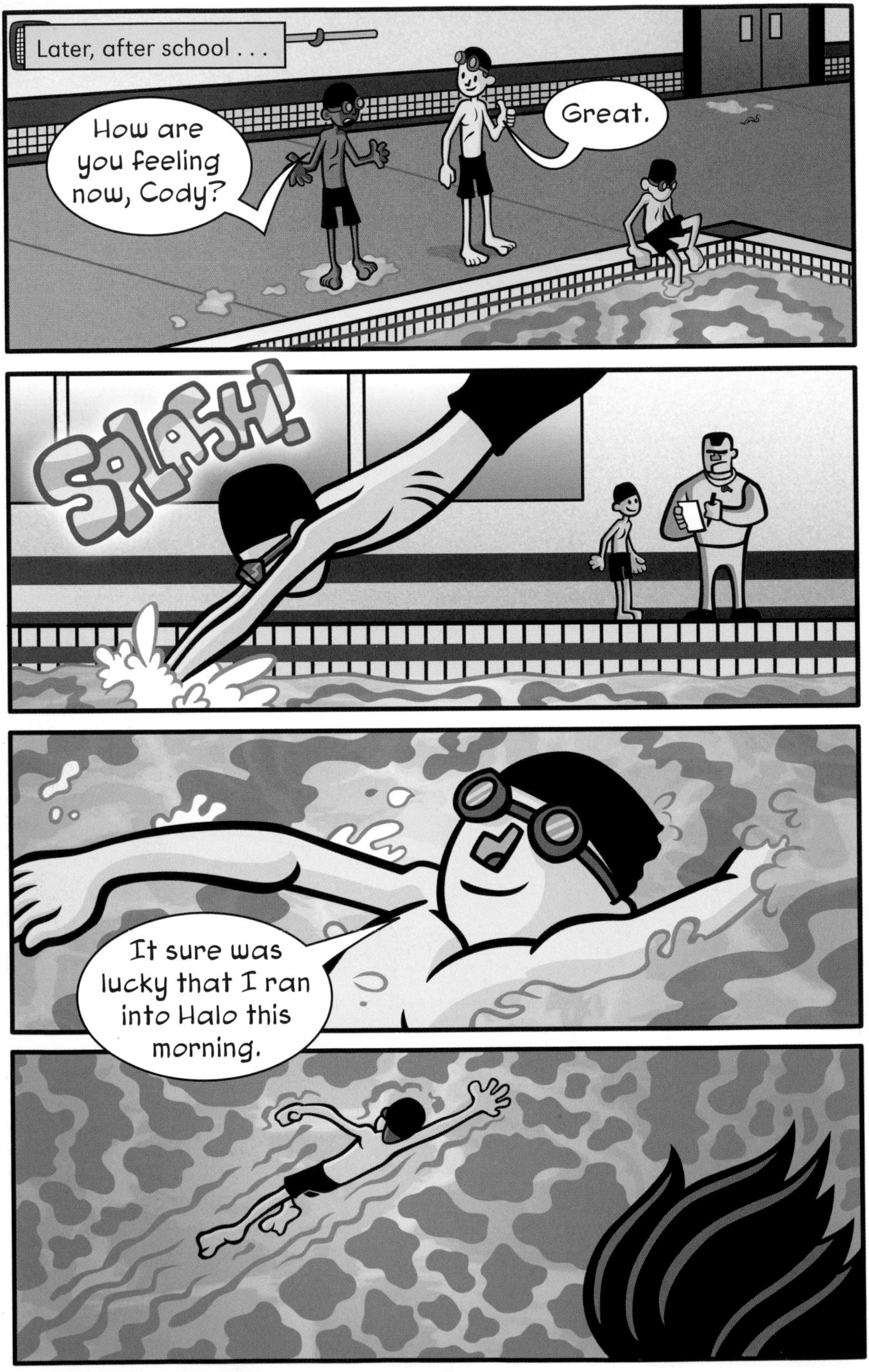

Later, after school . . .
How are you feeling now, Cody?
Great.
SPLASH!
It sure was lucky that I ran into Halo this morning.

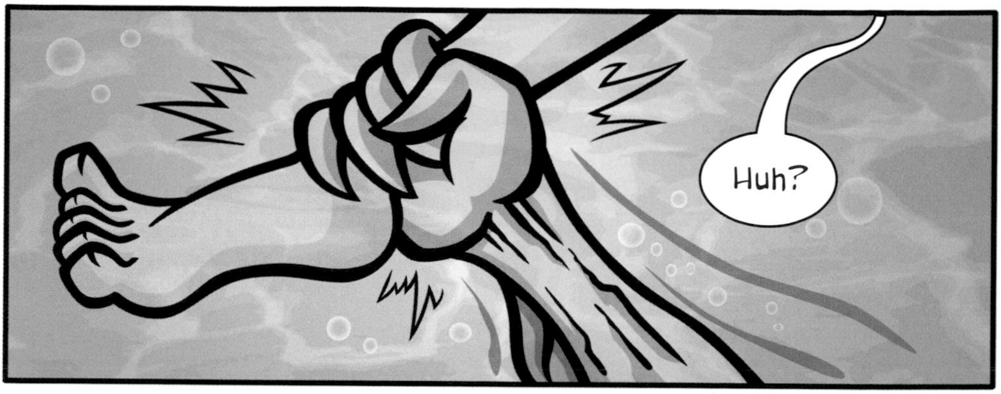
Huh?
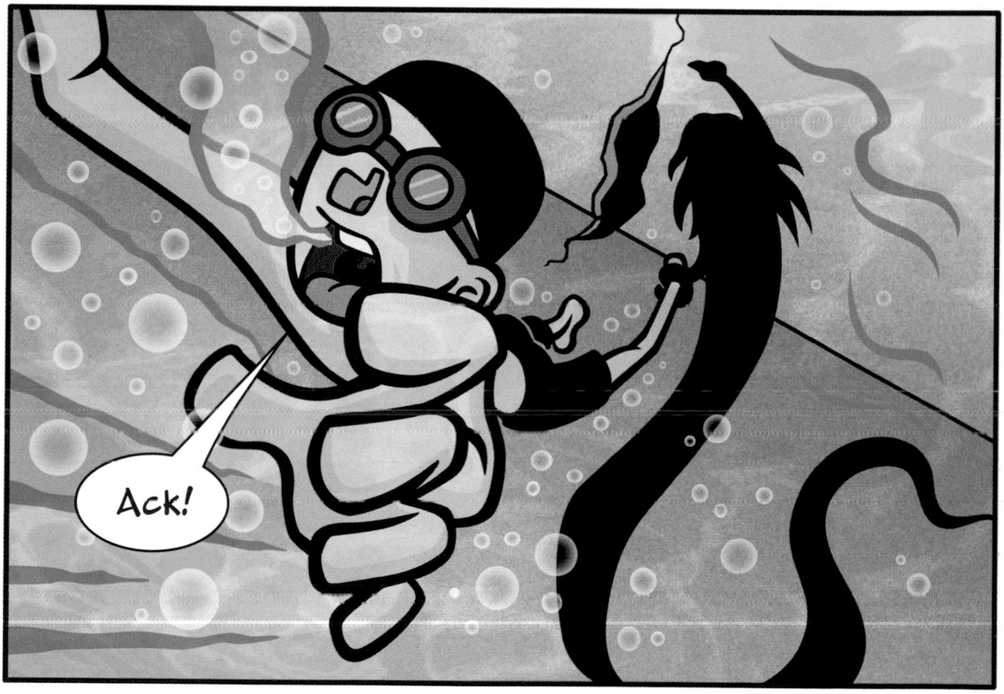
Ack!
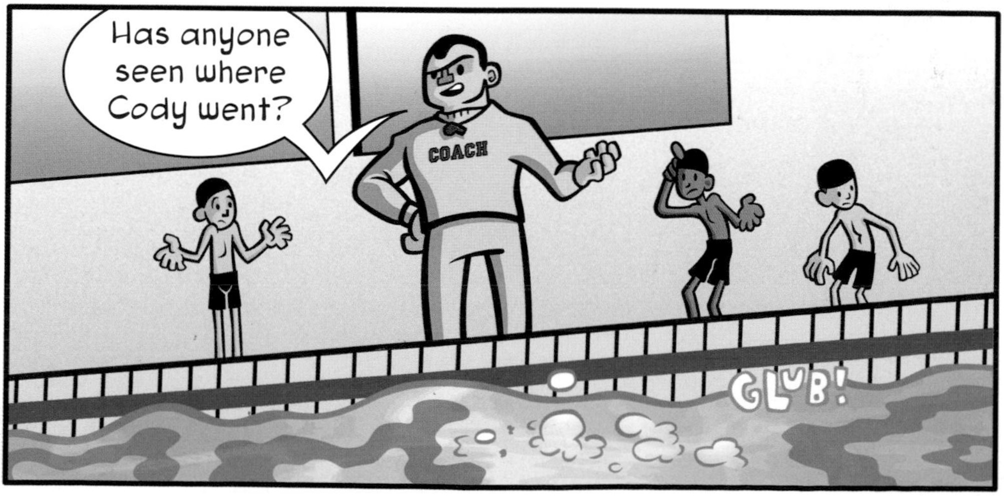
Has anyone seen where Cody went?
COACH
GLUB!

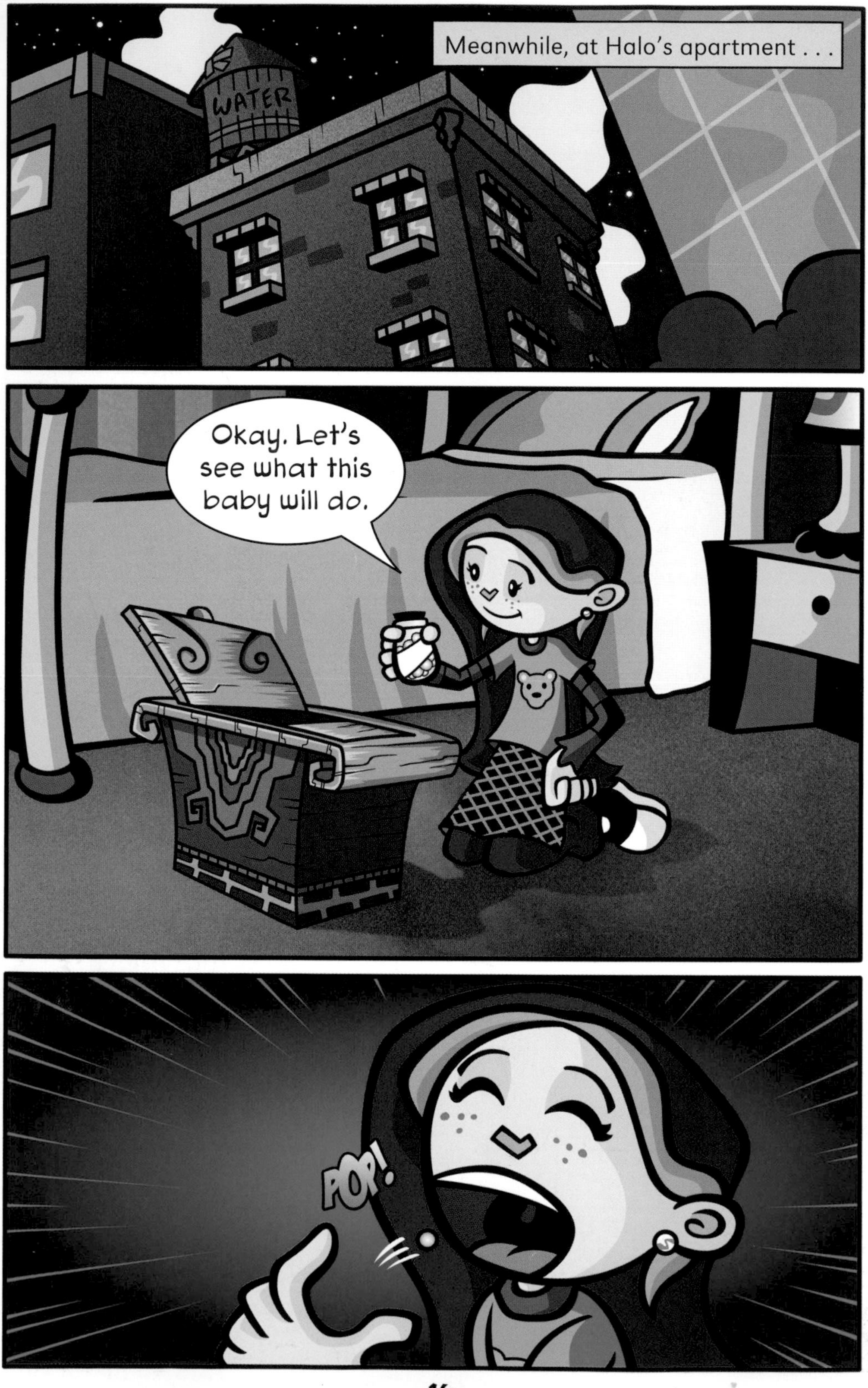
Meanwhile, at Halo's apartment . . .
WATER
Okay. Let's see what this baby will do.
POP!

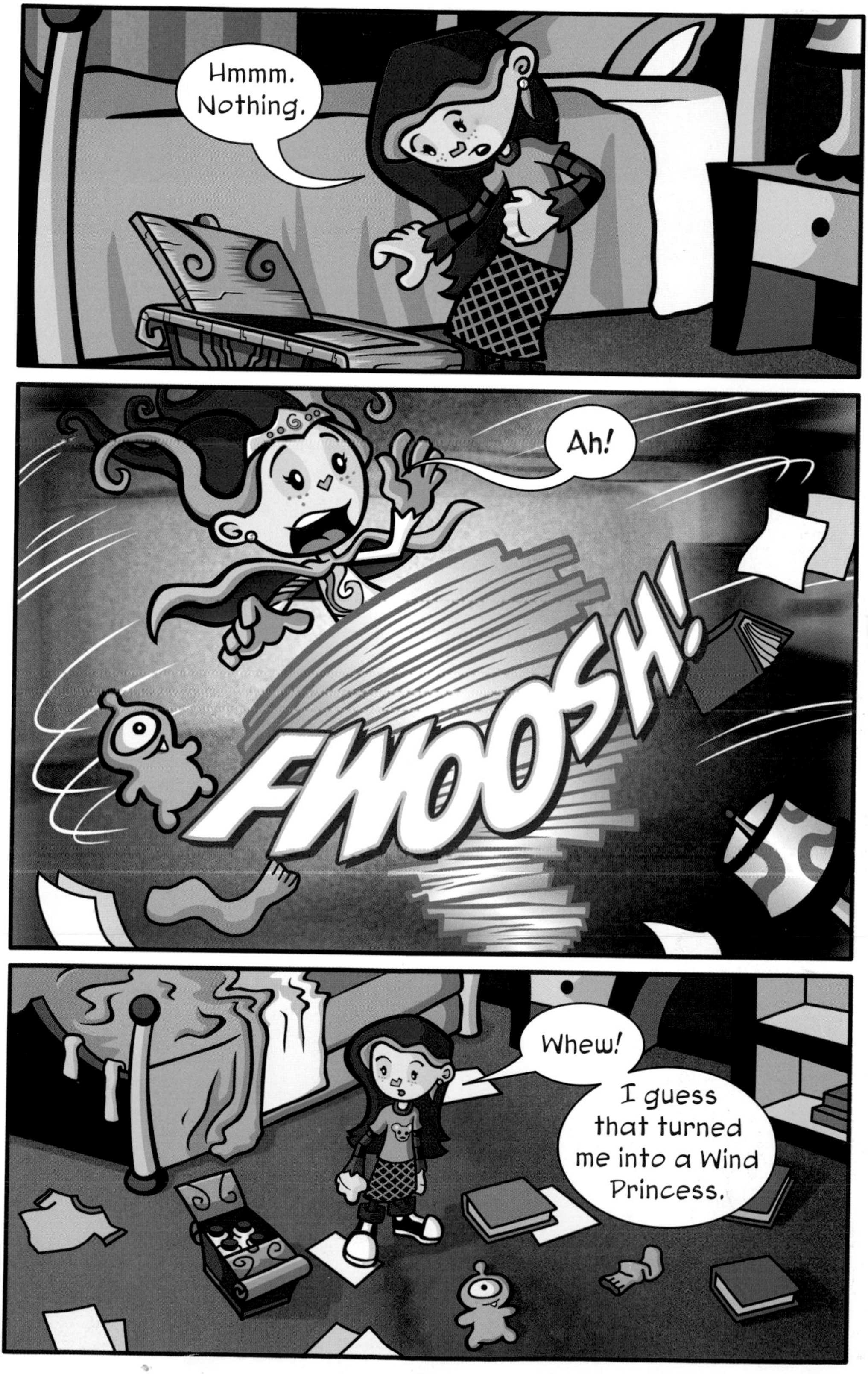
Hmmm. Nothing.
Ah!
FWOOSH!
Whew!
I guess that turned me into a Wind Princess.

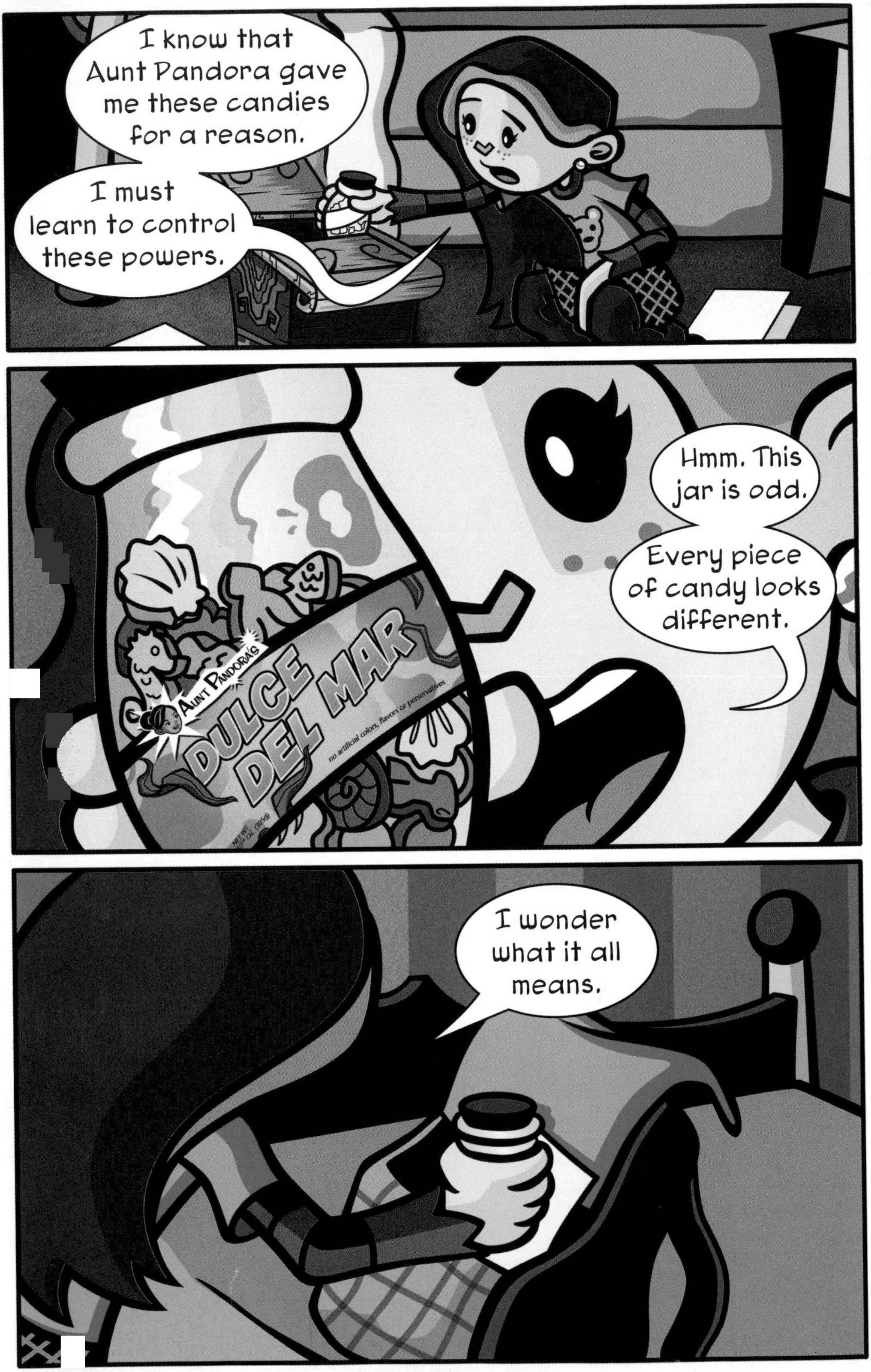
I know that Aunt Pandora gave me these candies for a reason.
I must learn to control these powers.
AUNT PANDORA'S
DULCE DEL MAR
no artificial colors, flavors or perservatives
Hmm. This jar is odd.
Every piece of candy looks different.
I wonder what it all means.

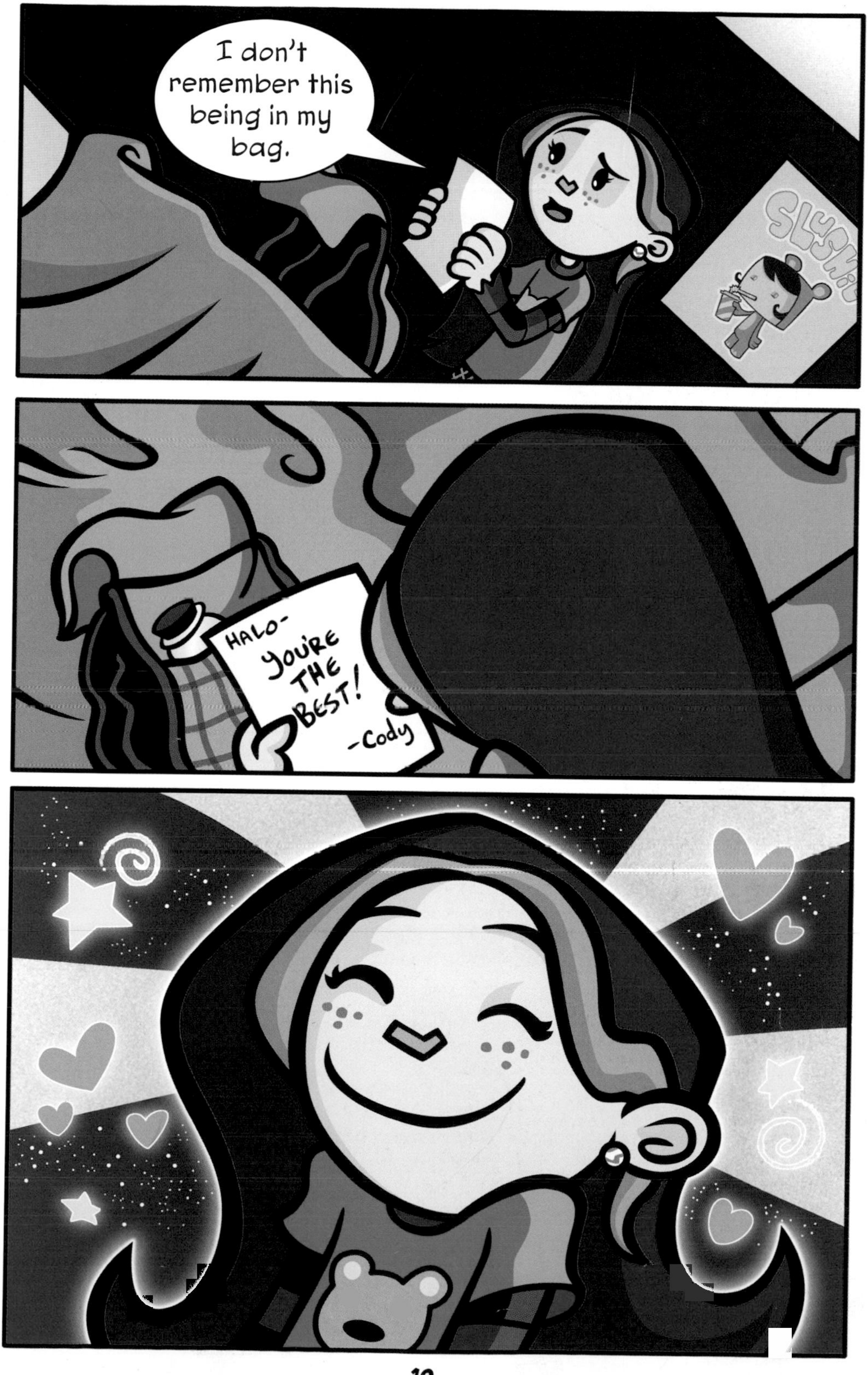
I don't remember this being in my bag.
SLUSH!
HALO-
YOU'RE THE BEST!
-Cody

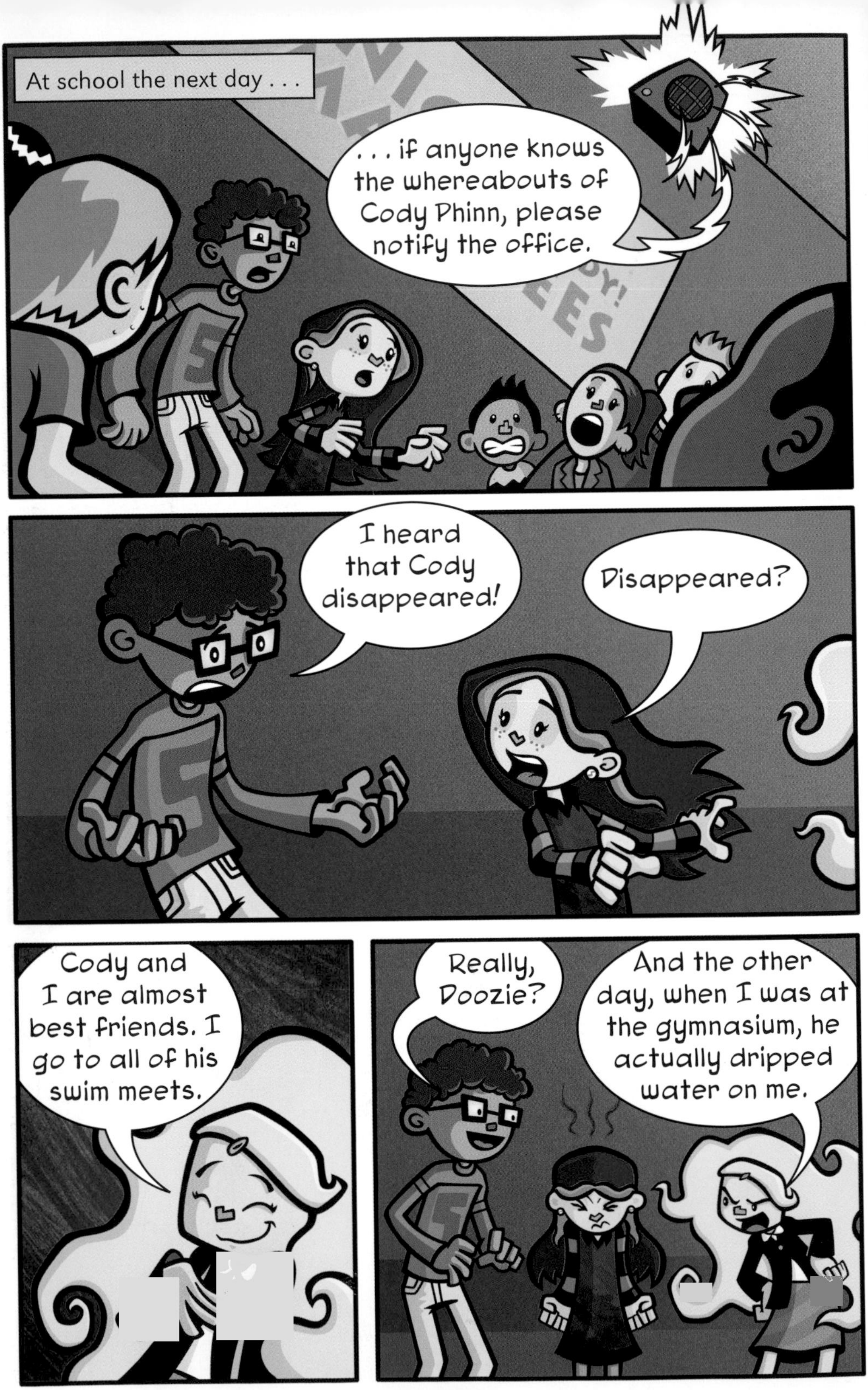
At school the next day . . .
. . . if anyone knows the whereabouts of Cody Phinn, please notify the office.
I heard that Cody disappeared!
Disappeared?
Cody and I are almost best friends. I go to all of his swim meets.
Really, Doozie?
And the other day, when I was at the gymnasium, he actually dripped water on me.

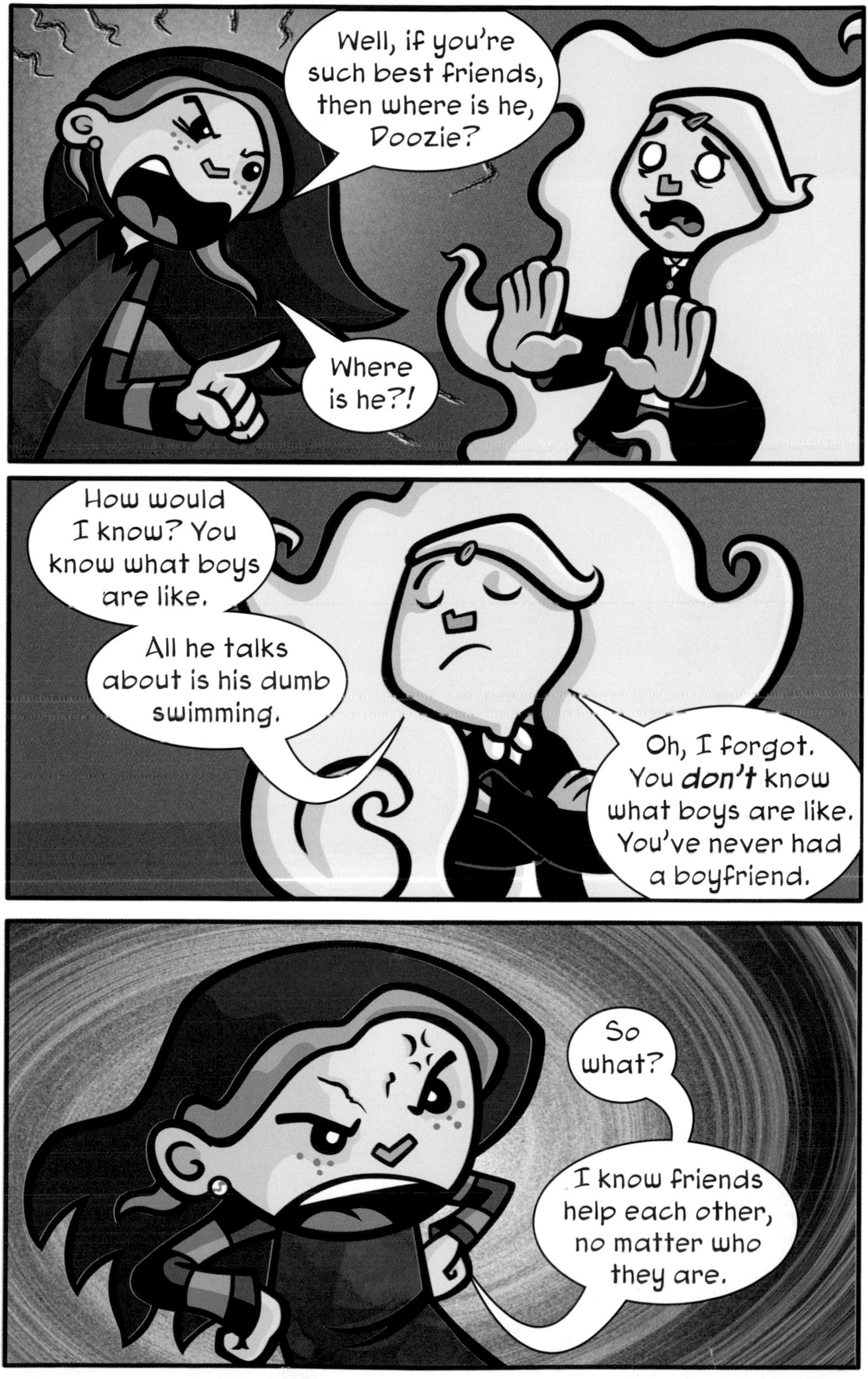
Well, if you're such best friends, then where is he, Doozie?
Where is he?!
How would I know? You know what boys are like.
All he talks about is his dumb swimming.
Oh, I forgot. You **don't** know what boys are like. You've never had a boyfriend.
So what?
I know friends help each other, no matter who they are.

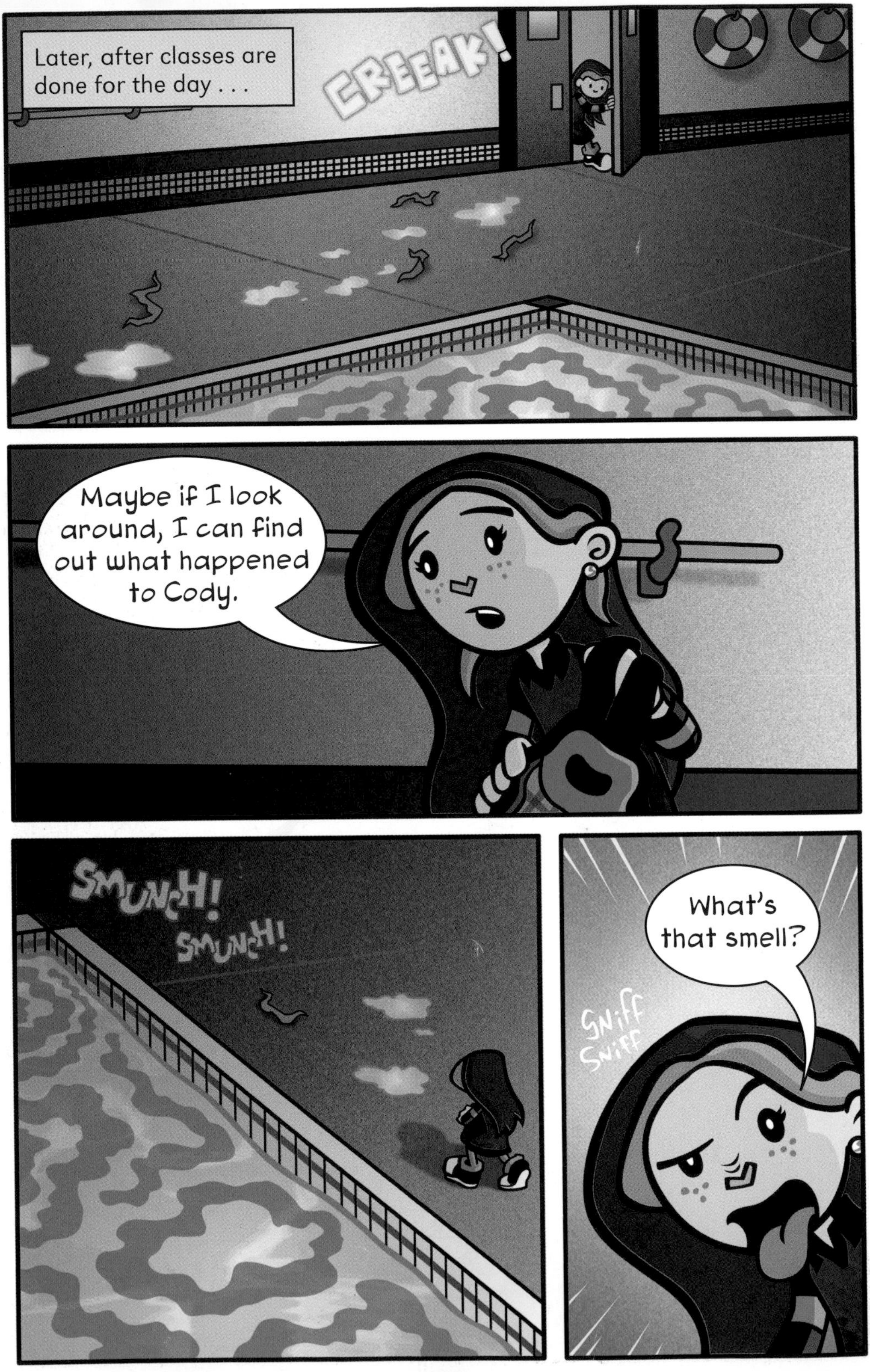
Later, after classes are done for the day . . .
CREEAK!
Maybe if I look around, I can find out what happened to Cody.
SMUNCH!
SMUNCH!
What's that smell?
SNIFF SNIFF

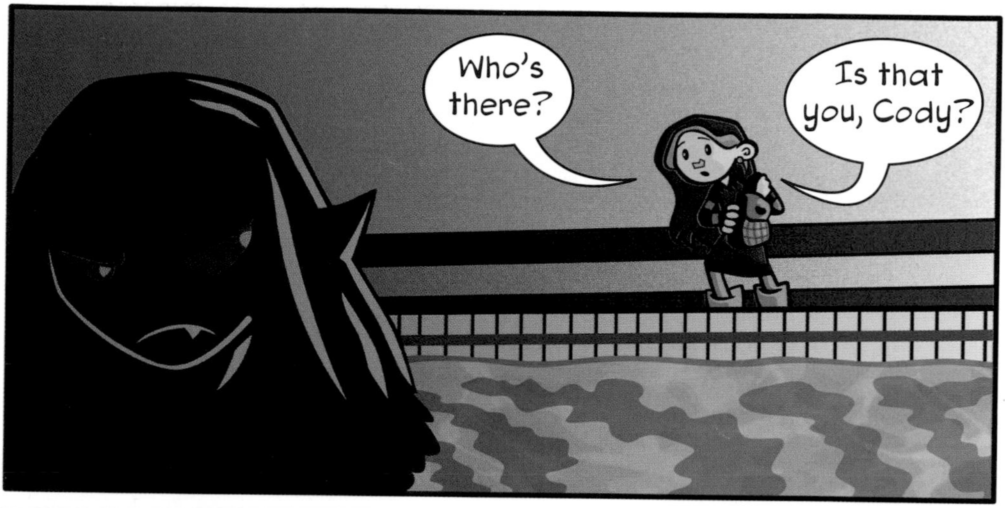
Who's there?
Is that you, Cody?

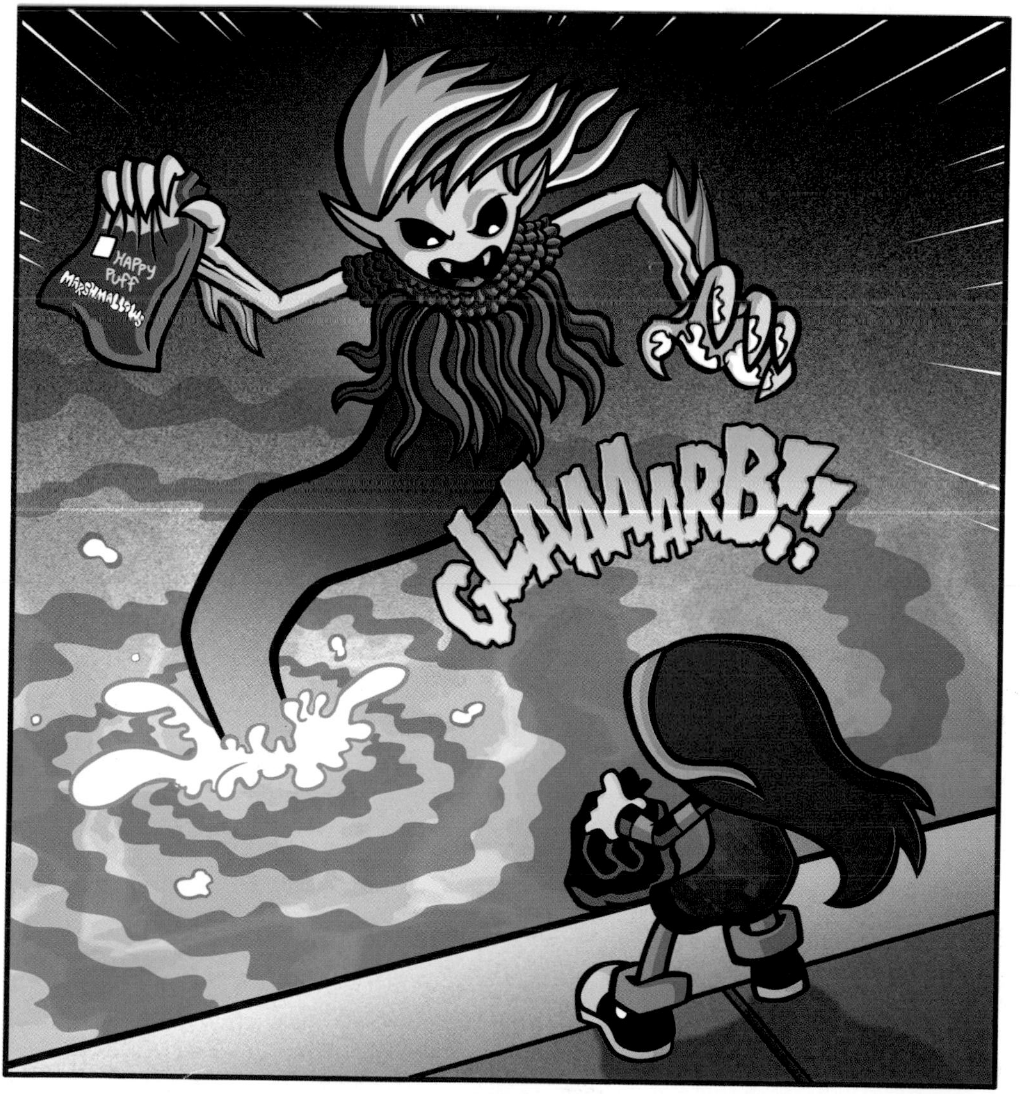
HAPPY PUFF MARSHMALLOWS
GLAAAARB!!

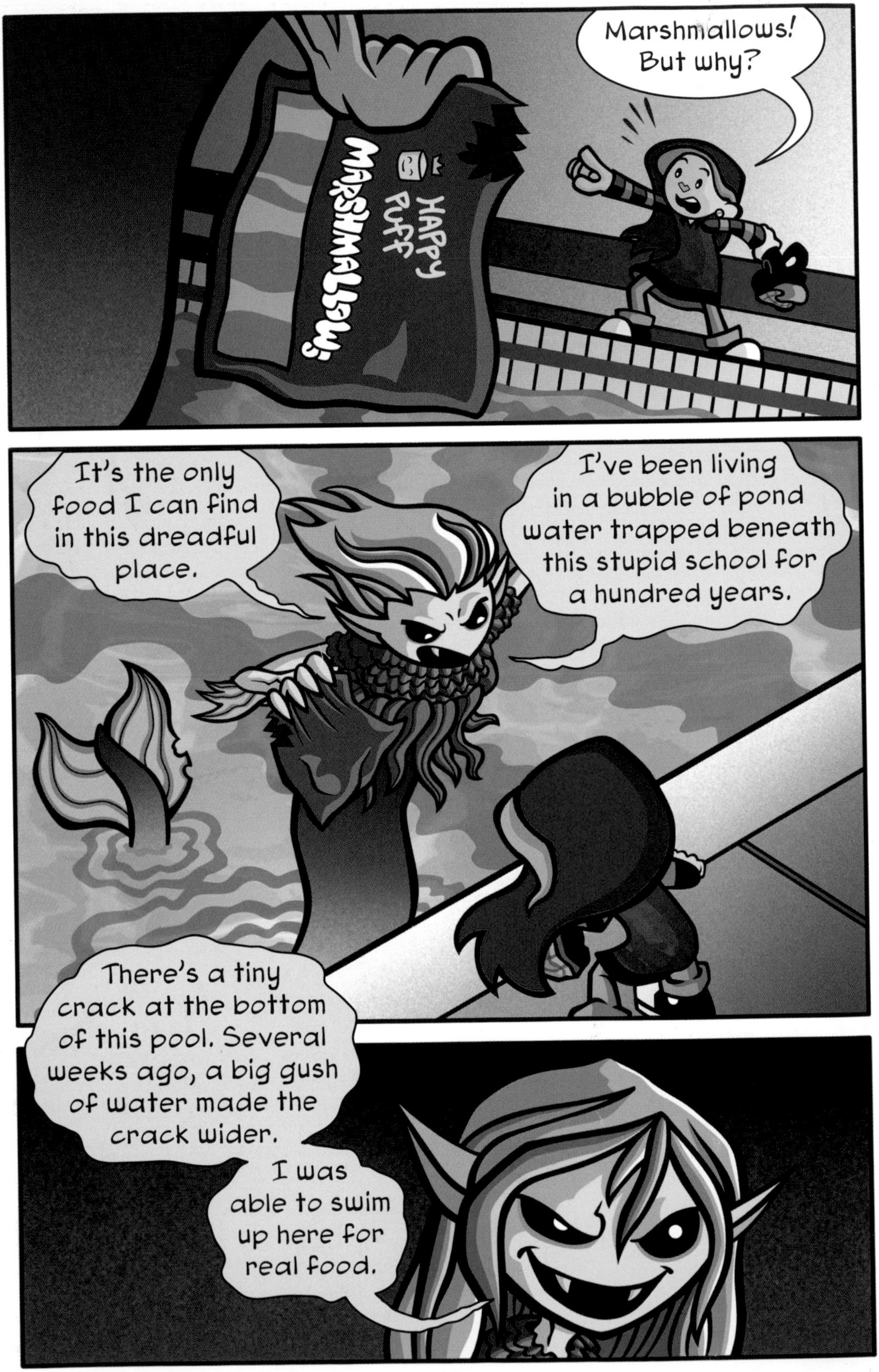
HAPPY PUFF MARSHMALLOWS
Marshmallows! But why?
It's the only food I can find in this dreadful place.
I've been living in a bubble of pond water trapped beneath this stupid school for a hundred years.
There's a tiny crack at the bottom of this pool. Several weeks ago, a big gush of water made the crack wider.
I was able to swim up here for real food.

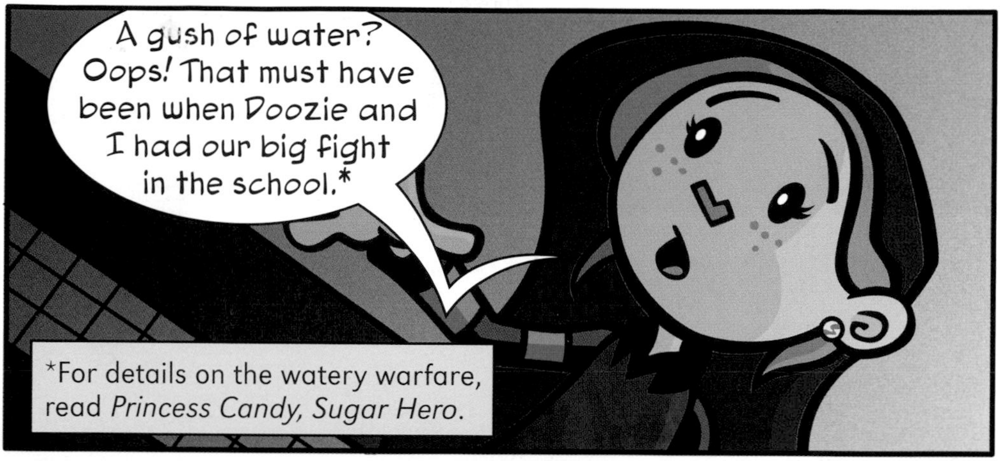
A gush of water? Oops! That must have been when Doozie and I had our big fight in the school.*
*For details on the watery warfare, read *Princess Candy, Sugar Hero*.

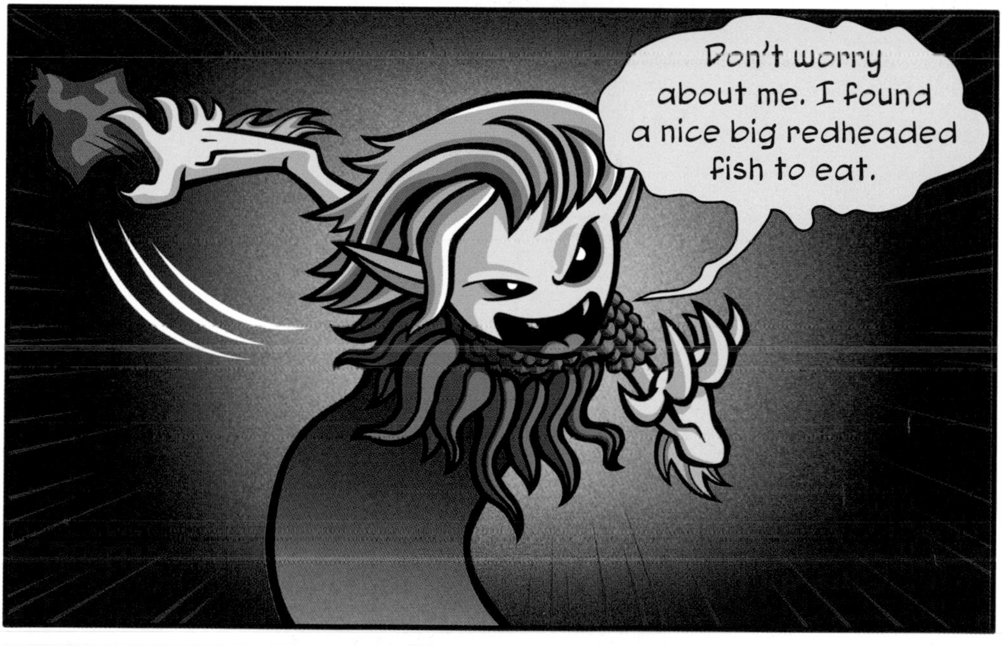
Don't worry about me. I found a nice big redheaded fish to eat.

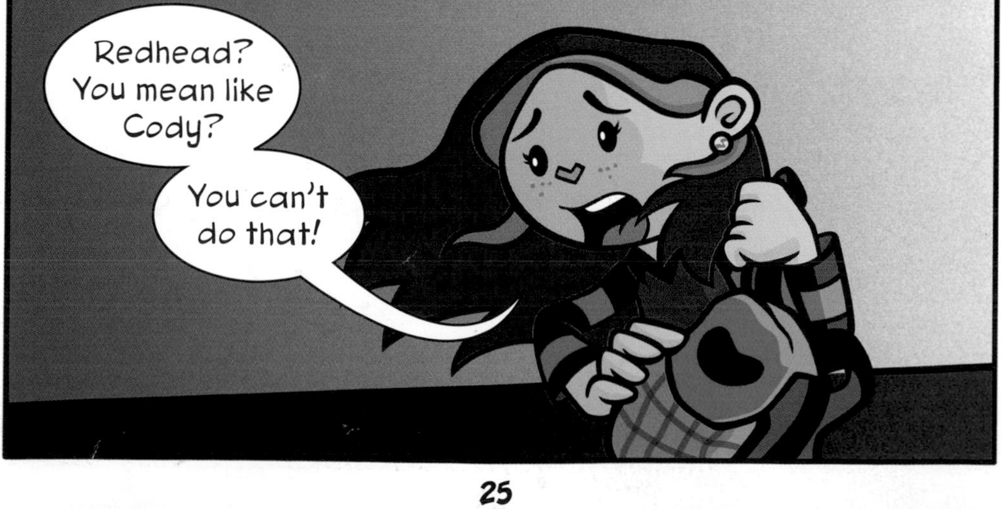
Redhead? You mean like Cody?
You can't do that!

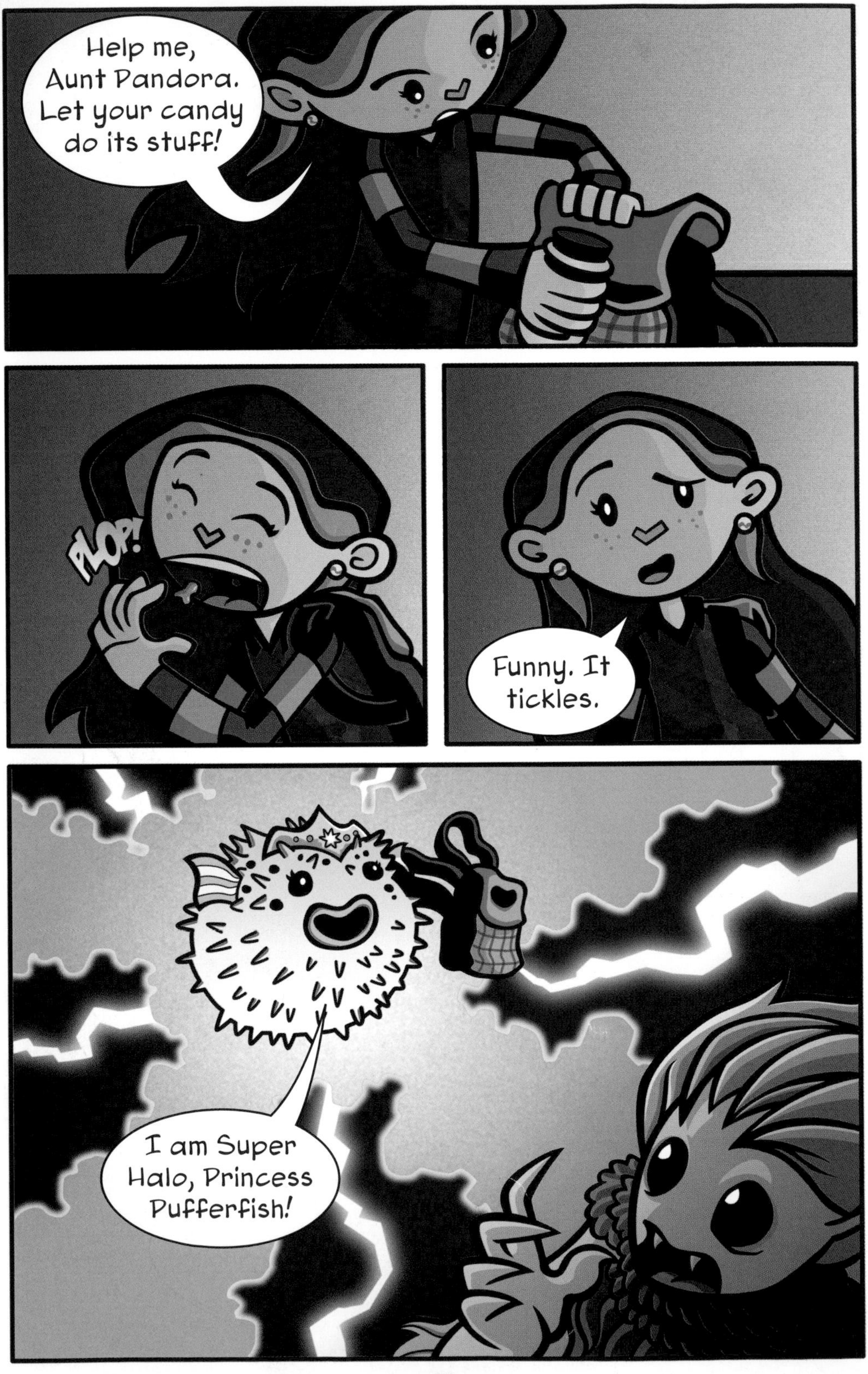
Help me, Aunt Pandora. Let your candy do its stuff!
PLOP!
Funny. It tickles.
I am Super Halo, Princess Pufferfish!

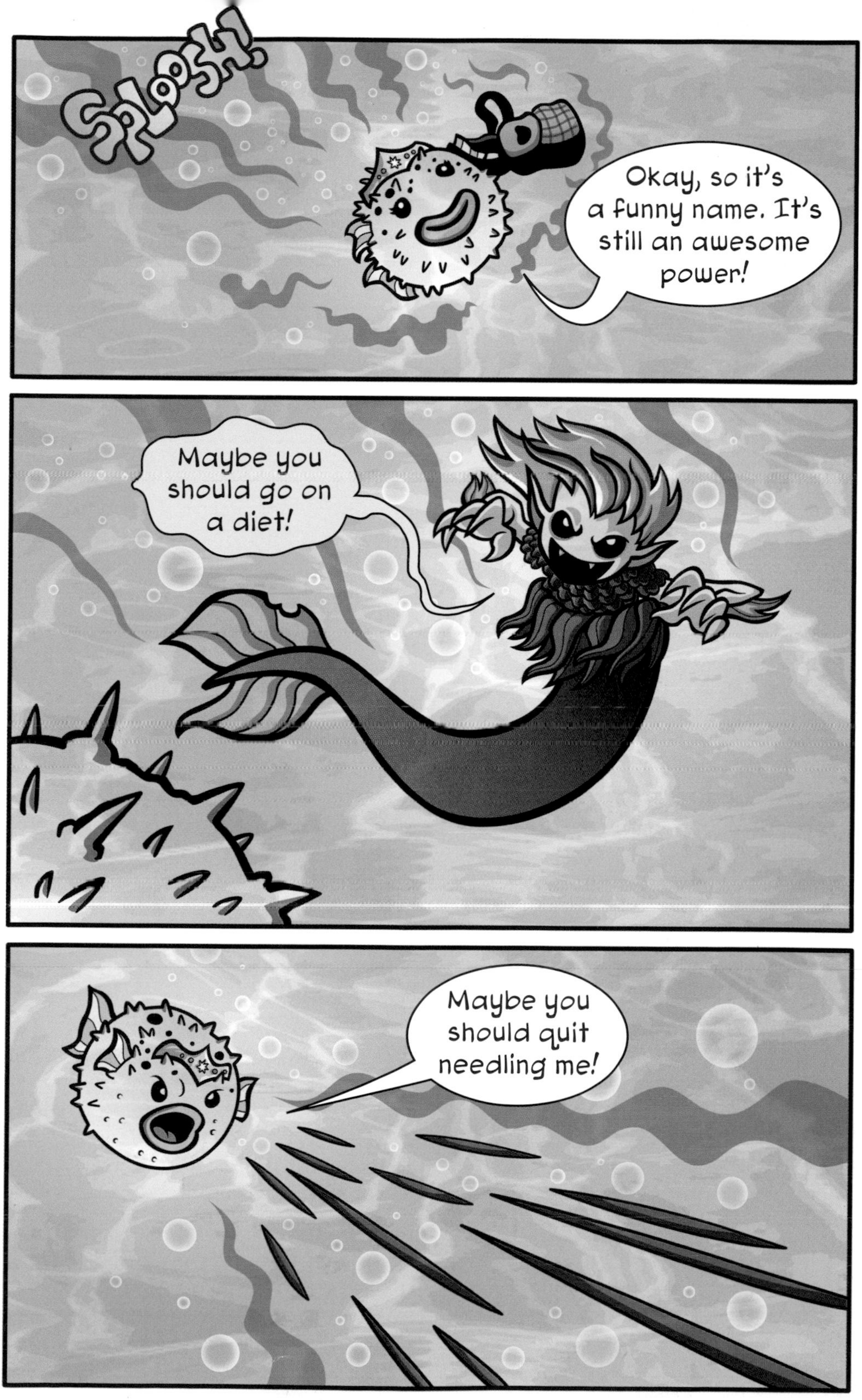
SPLOOSH!
Okay, so it's a funny name. It's still an awesome power!
Maybe you should go on a diet!
Maybe you should quit needling me!

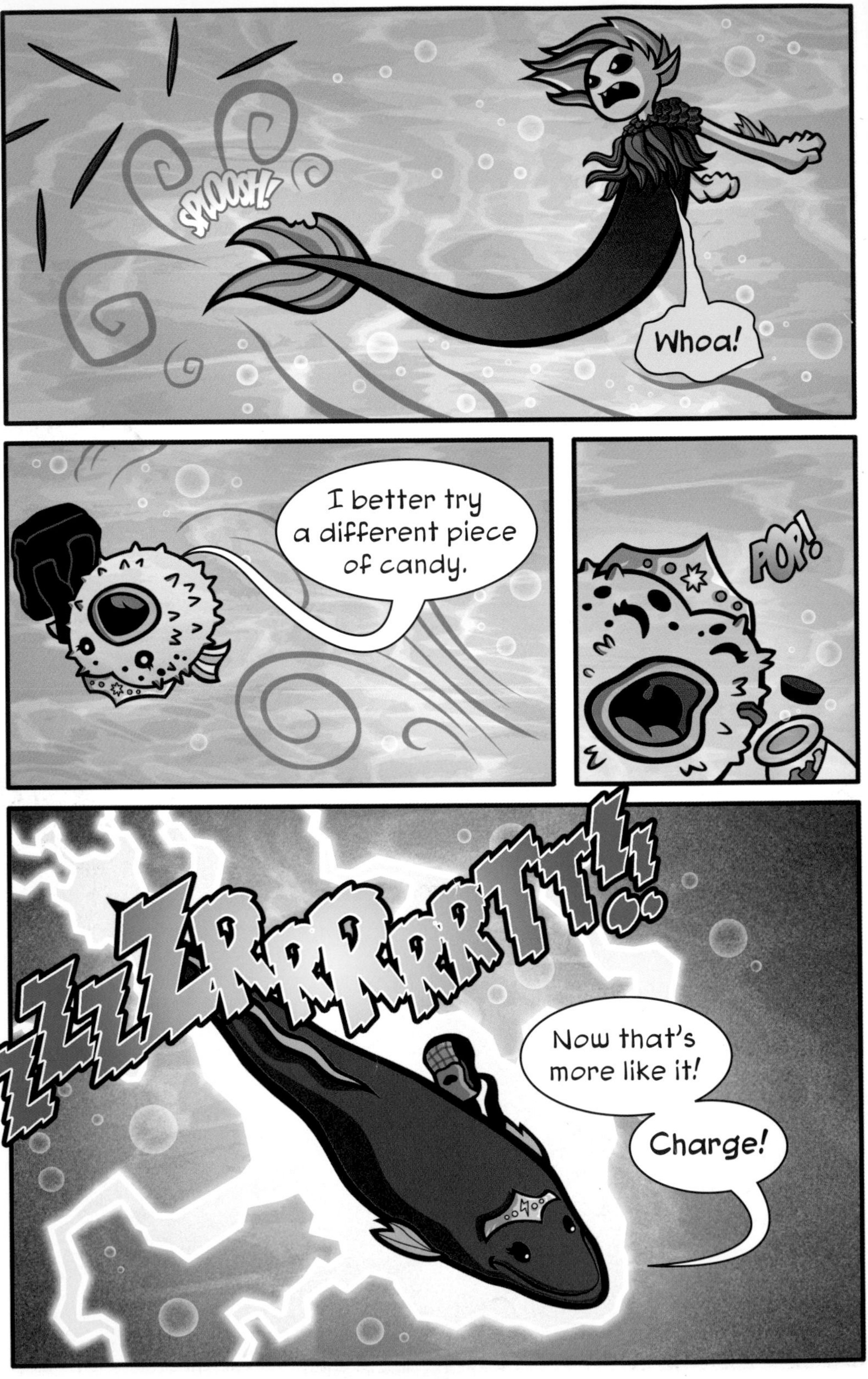
SPLOOSH!
Whoa!
I better try a different piece of candy.
POP!
ZZZZRRRRRRTTT!!
Now that's more like it!
Charge!

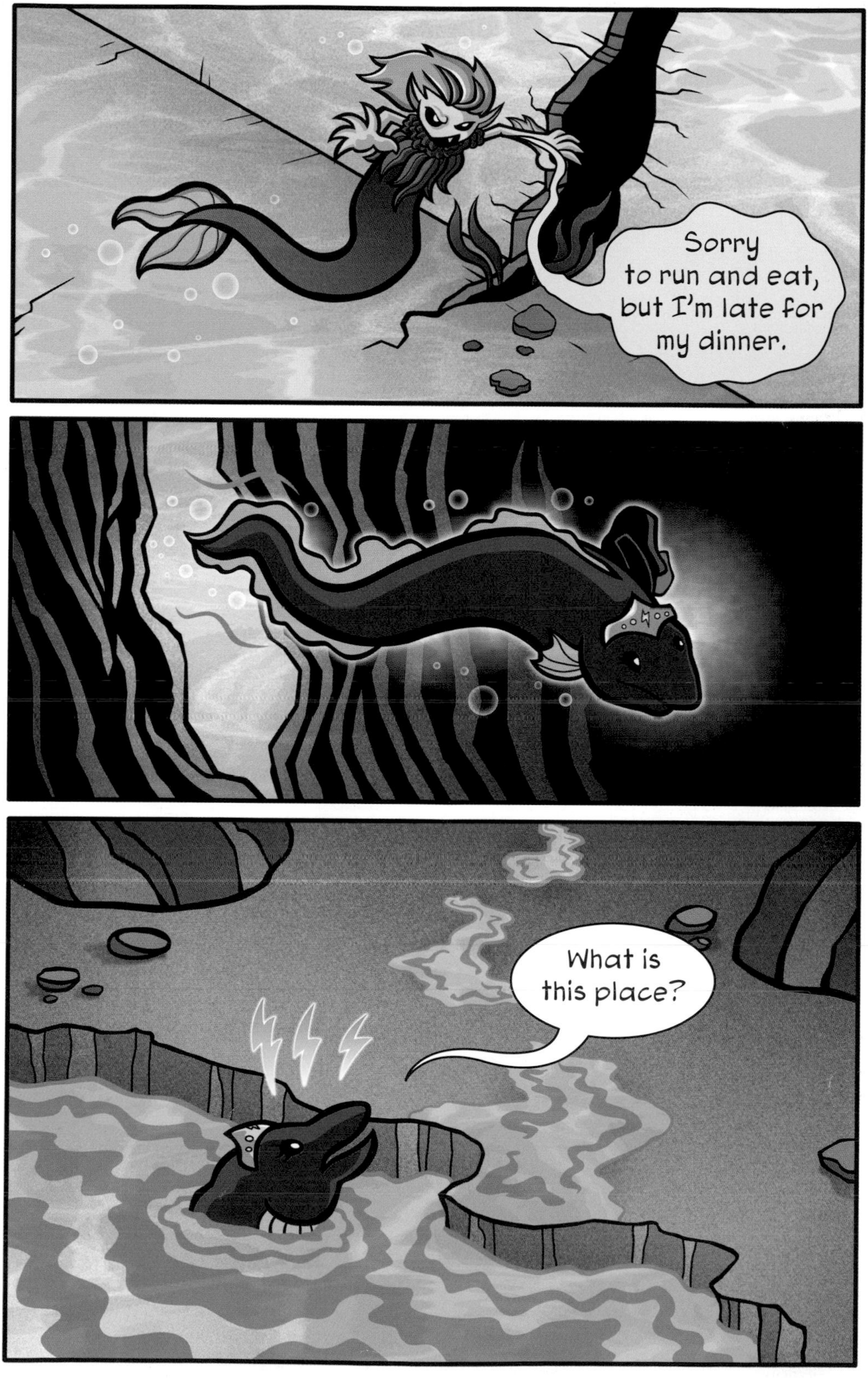
Sorry to run and eat, but I'm late for my dinner.
What is this place?

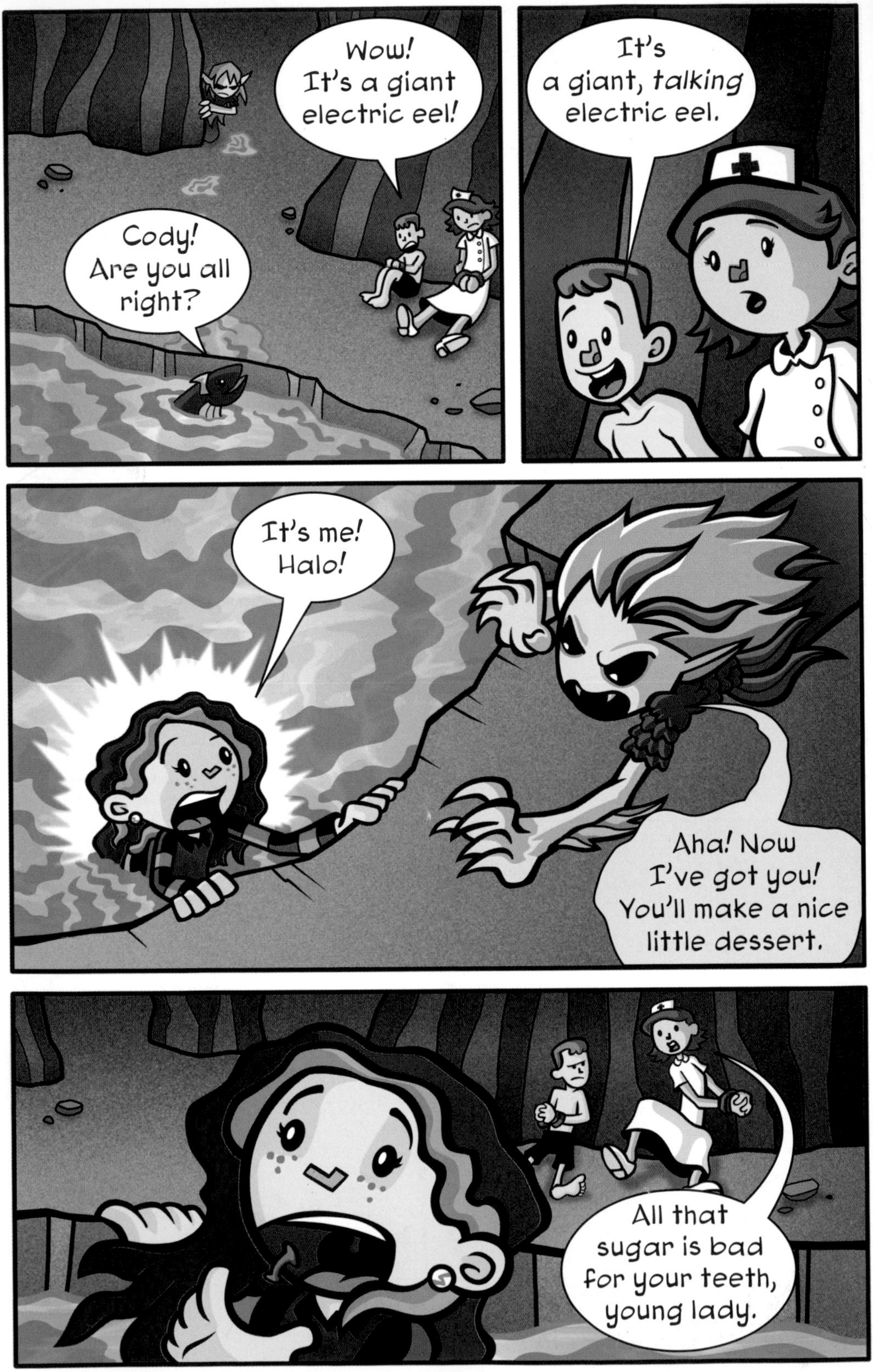
Wow! It's a giant electric eel!
Cody! Are you all right?
It's a giant, *talking* electric eel.
It's me! Halo!
Aha! Now I've got you! You'll make a nice little dessert.
All that sugar is bad for your teeth, young lady.

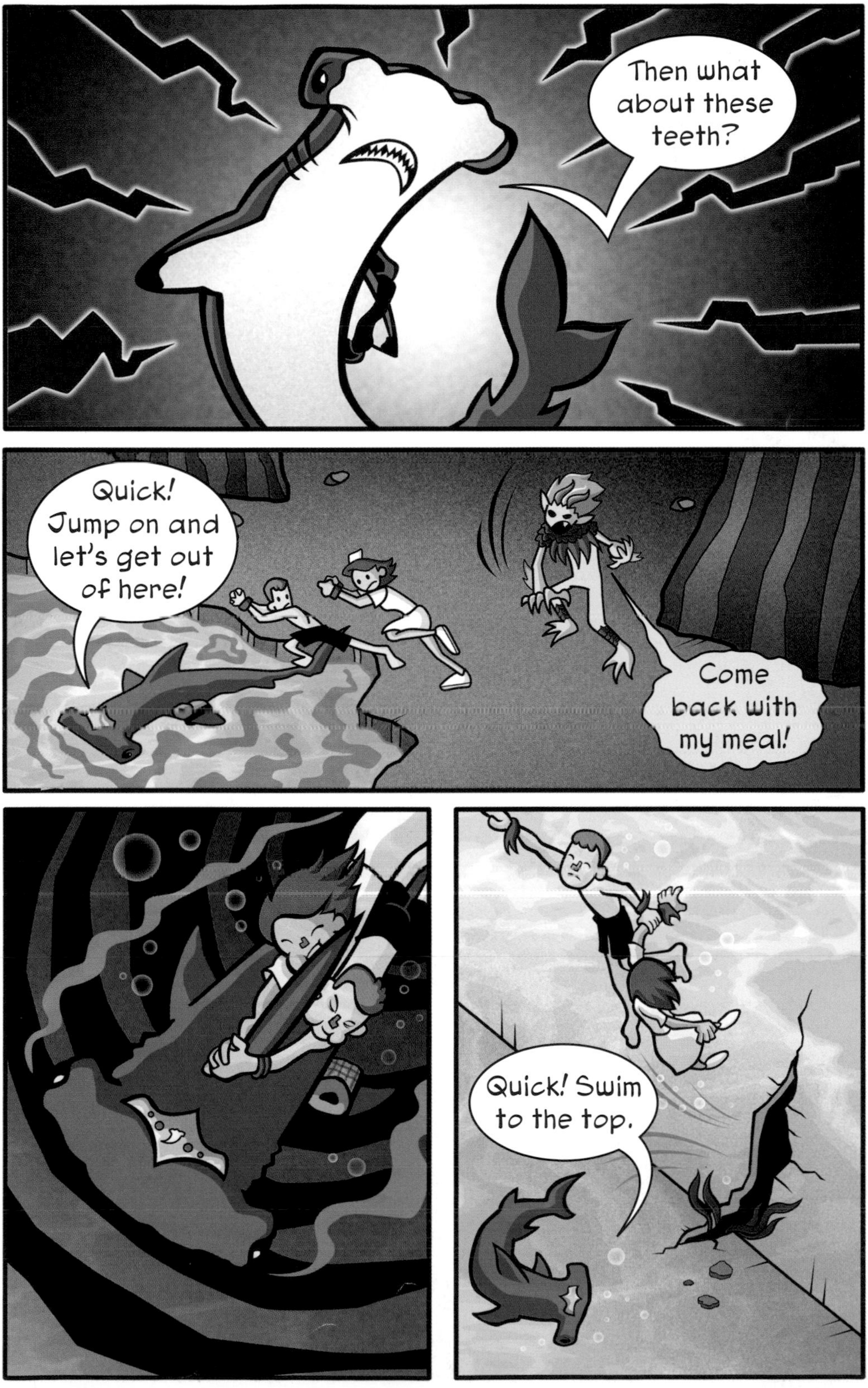
Then what about these teeth?
Quick! Jump on and let's get out of here!
Come back with my meal!
Quick! Swim to the top.

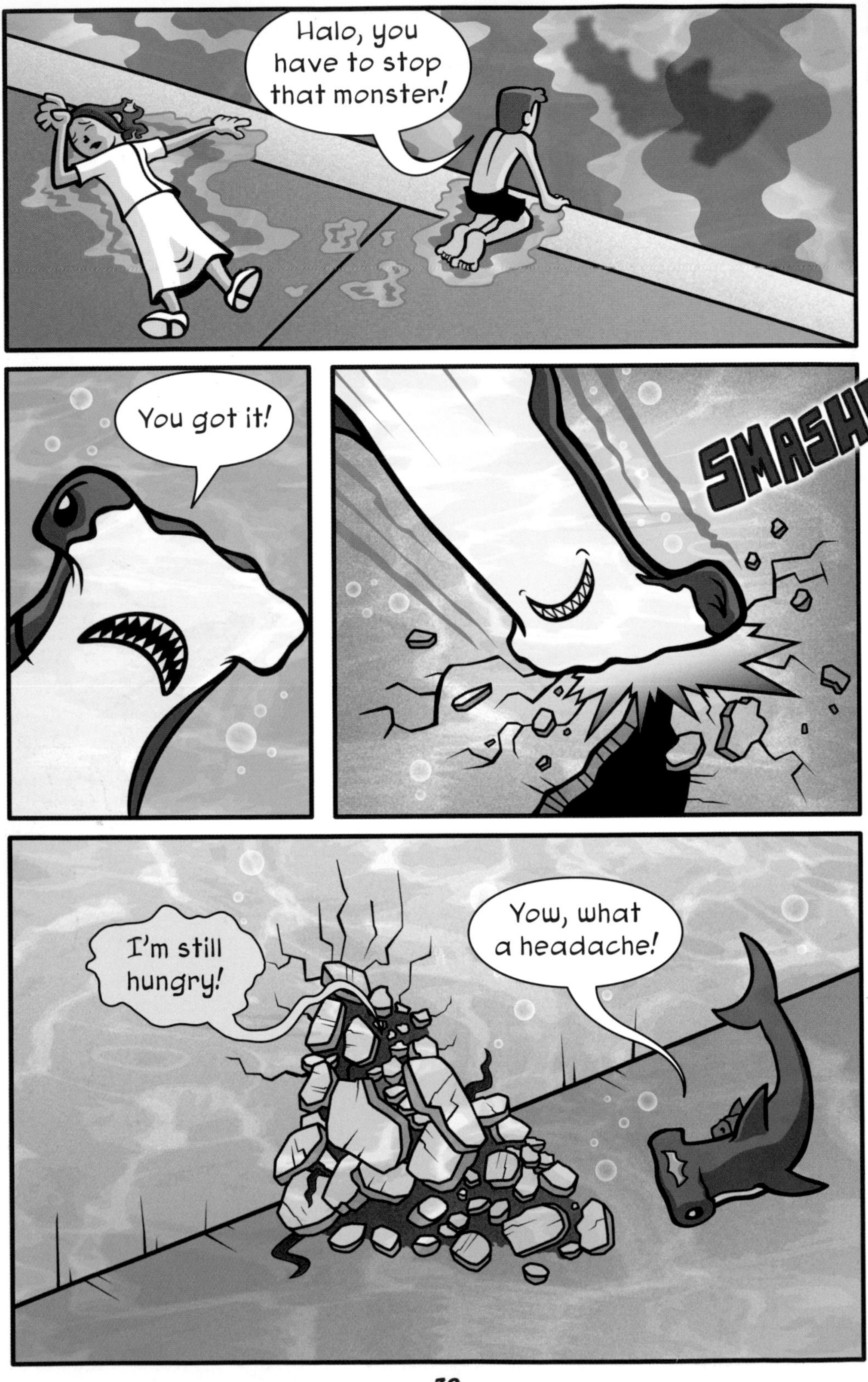
Halo, you have to stop that monster!
You got it!
SMASH
I'm still hungry!
You, what a headache!

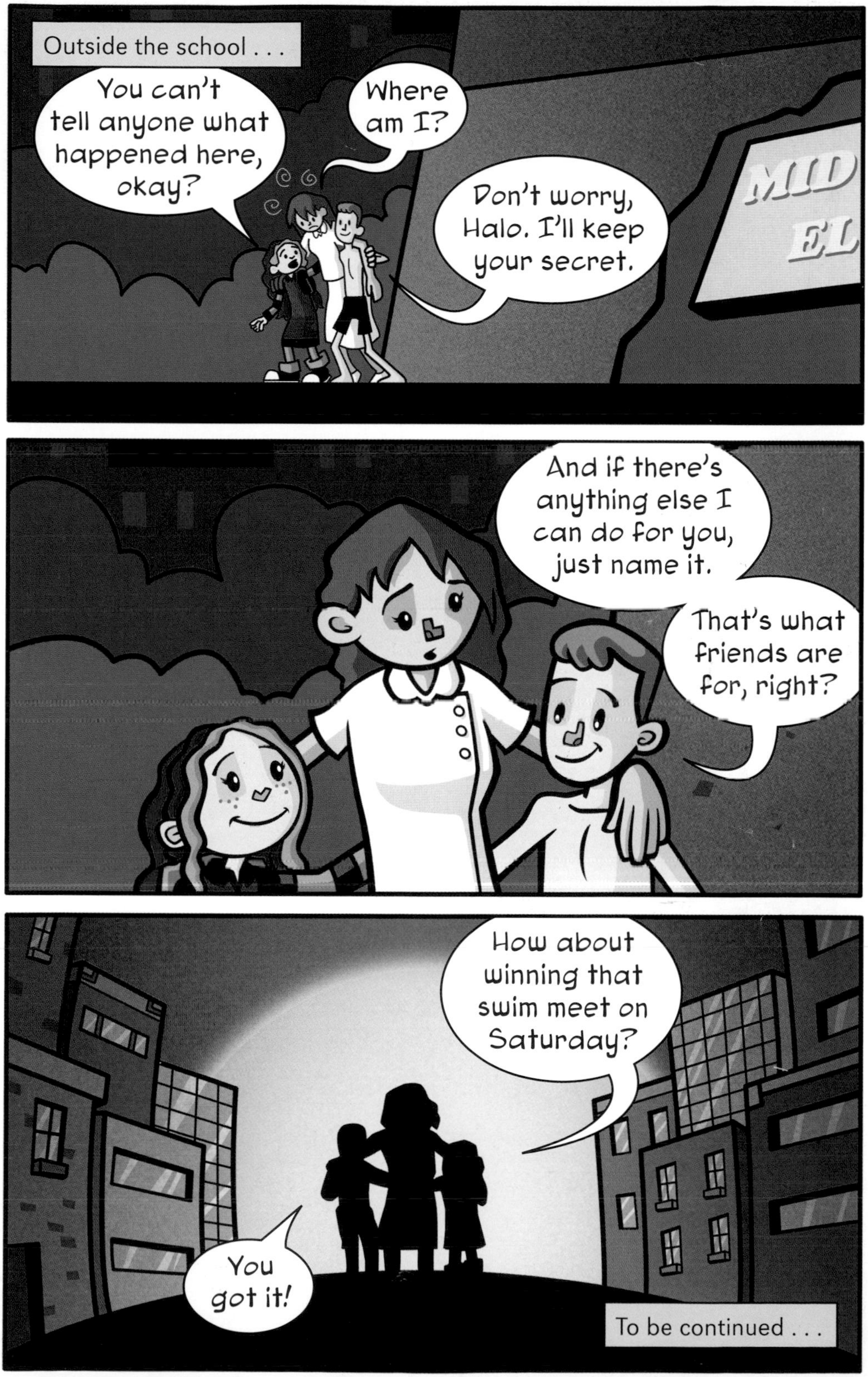
Outside the school . . .
You can't tell anyone what happened here, okay?
Where am I?
Don't worry, Halo. I'll keep your secret.
MID
EL
And if there's anything else I can do for you, just name it.
That's what friends are for, right?
How about winning that swim meet on Saturday?
You got it!
To be continued . . .

About The Author

Michael Dahl is the author of more than 200 books for children and young adults. He has won the AEP Distinguished Achievement Award three times for his non-fiction. His Finnegan Zwake mystery series was shortlisted twice by the Anthony and Agatha awards. He has also written the Library of Doom series and the Dragonblood books. He is a featured speaker at conferences around the country on graphic novels and high-interest books for boys.

About The Illustrator

Jeff Crowther has been drawing comics for as long as he can remember. Since graduating from college, Jeff has worked on a variety of illustrations for clients including Disney, Adventures Magazine, and Boy's Life Magazine. He also wrote and illustrated the webcomic Sketchbook and has self-published several mini-comics. Jeff lives in Boardman, Ohio, with his wife, Elizabeth, and their children, Jonas and Noelle.

Glossary

active ingredients (AK-tiv in-GREE-dee-uhnts)—the main items that something is made from

allergic (uh-LUR-jik)—if you are allergic to something, it can cause a reaction, such as a rash, sneezing, or sickness

apartment (uh-PART-muhnt)—rooms inside a larger building that are rented as a home

dreadful (DRED-fuhl)—very bad

gelatin (JEL-uh-tuhn)—a clear substance often used for making jelly or desserts

gush (GUHSH)—to flow quickly in large amounts

gymnasium (jim-NAY-zee-uhm)—a gym, or a large room with equipment for exercises and sports

practical joke (PRAK-tuh-kuhl JOKE)—a prank intended to trick or embarrass someone

whereabouts (WAIR-uh-bouts)—roughly where someone or something is located

MarshMallow MerMaid

SUPER-VILLAIN

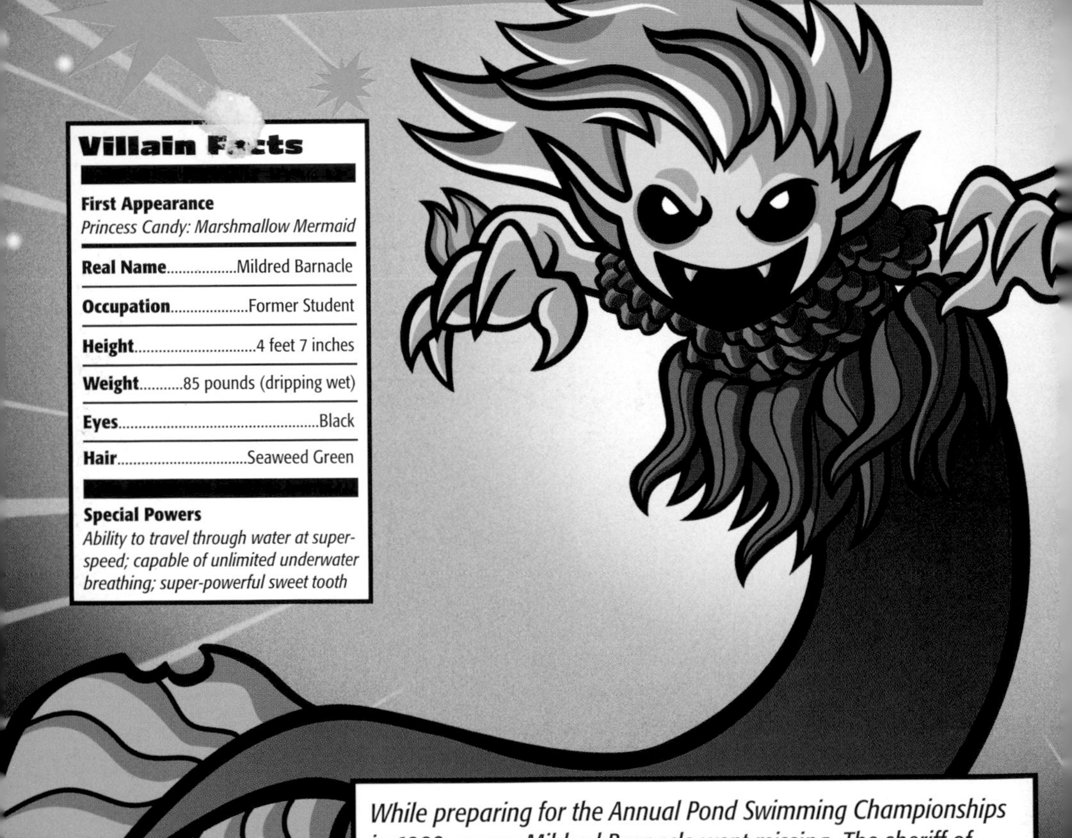

Villain Facts

First Appearance
Princess Candy: Marshmallow Mermaid

Real Name.................Mildred Barnacle

Occupation..................Former Student

Height...............................4 feet 7 inches

Weight...........85 pounds (dripping wet)

Eyes...Black

Hair................................Seaweed Green

Special Powers
Ability to travel through water at super-speed; capable of unlimited underwater breathing; super-powerful sweet tooth

While preparing for the Annual Pond Swimming Championships in 1889, young Mildred Barnacle went missing. The sheriff of Midnight searched the town for months, but Mildred was never found. A decade later, workers drained the local wateringhole and built Midnight Elementary in its place. For a hundred years, students passed through the school's doors, unaware of what lay beneath. Then one day, a crack in the swimming pool allowed Mildred to emerge from her watery grave. She had become the slippery and sweet-toothed . . . Marshmallow Mermaid!

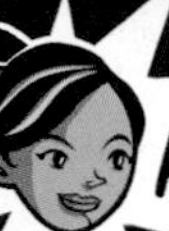

Aunt Pandora's

Princess Puzzlers

Q: Who ate the first marshmallows?

A: Believe it or not, ancient Egyptian royalty snacked on marshmallows more than 4,000 years ago.

Q: Where did marshmallows get their funny name?

A: Egyptians made the first marshmallows from "mallow" plants, which are often found in swampy "marshes."

Q: How big was the largest s'more ever made?

A: Built in 2003, the world's largest s'more weighed 1,600 pounds and contained 20,000 toasted marshmallows!

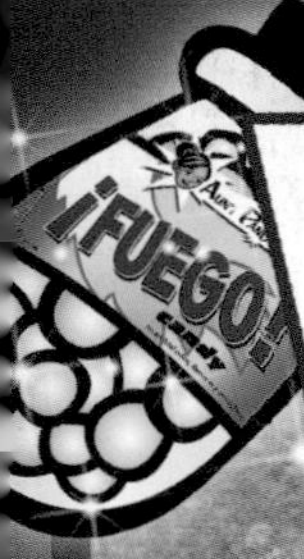
¡FUEGO!
candy

Discussion Question

1. Cody is allergic to marshmallows. Are you allergic to any types of food? If so, how do you deal with your allergy? If not, have you ever met anyone with a food allergy?

2. If Doozie Hiss was captured by the Marshmallow Mermaid, do you think Halo would save her? Why or why not?

3. At the end of the story, Halo escapes the Marshmallow Mermaid. Do you think the evil fish will ever return to Midnight Elementary? Why or why not?

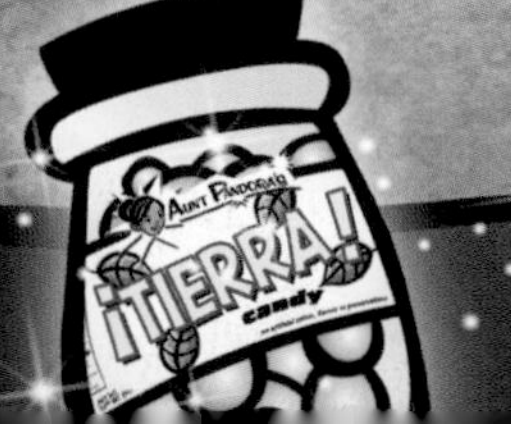
Aunt Pandora's
¡TIERRA!
candy

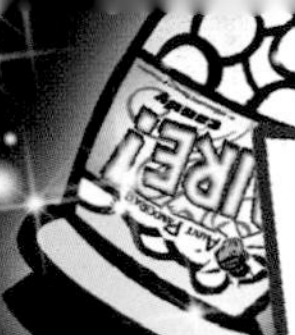

Writing Prompts

1. Pretend your favorite candy could turn you into a superhero. What would your superhero name be? What superpowers would you have? How would you use those powers?

2. Imagine you are the author and write a second part to this story. Does the Marshmallow Mermaid come back? Does Cody win his swim race?

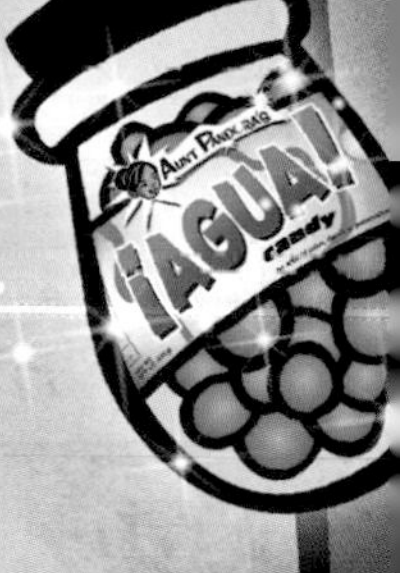
¡AGUA!
candy

3. Comics and graphic novels are often written and illustrated by two different people. Write a short story, and then give it to a friend to draw the pictures.

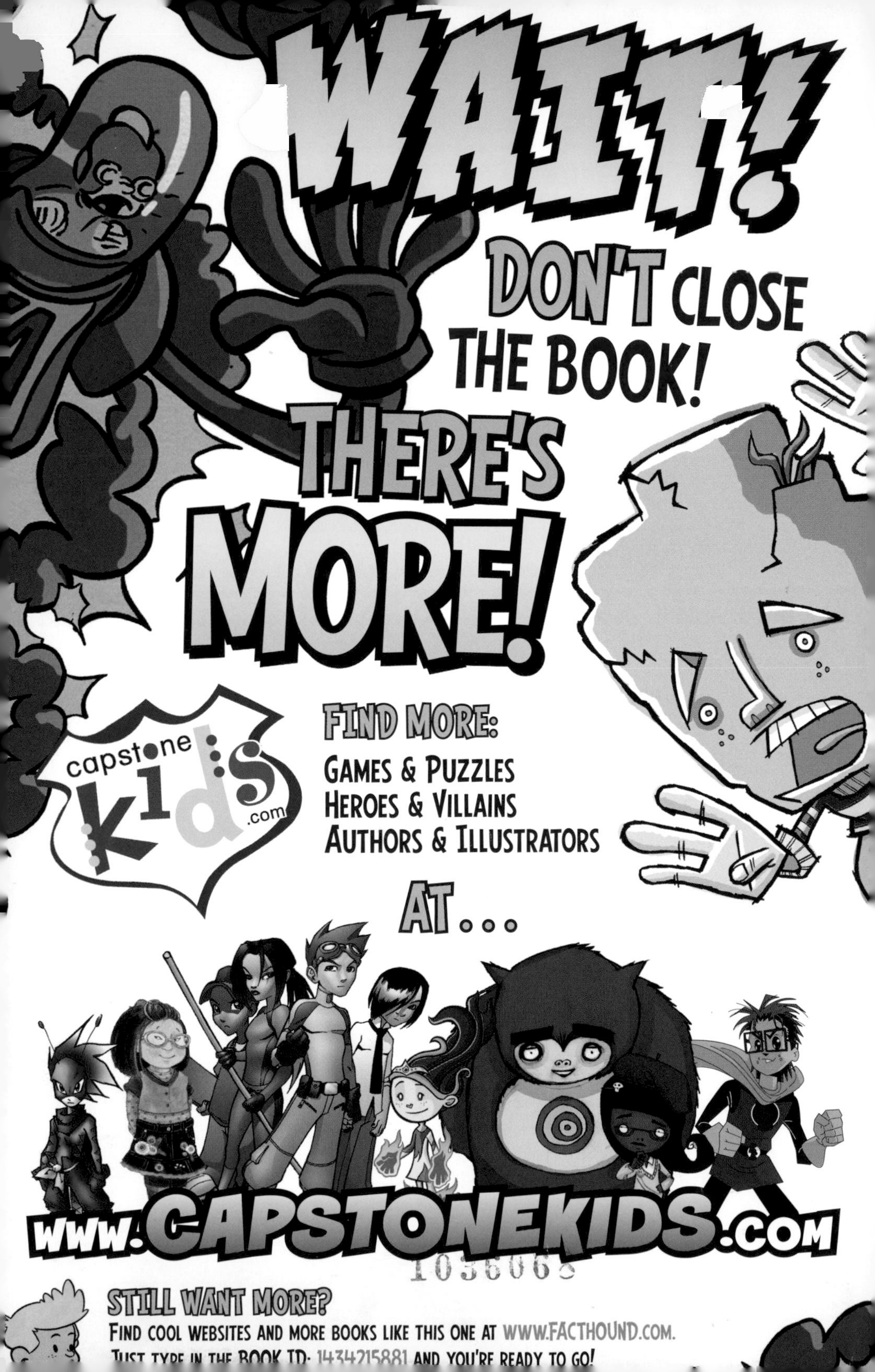
WAIT!
DON'T CLOSE THE BOOK!
THERE'S MORE!
capstone kids .com
FIND MORE:
GAMES & PUZZLES
HEROES & VILLAINS
AUTHORS & ILLUSTRATORS
AT...
WWW.CAPSTONEKIDS.COM
STILL WANT MORE?
FIND COOL WEBSITES AND MORE BOOKS LIKE THIS ONE AT WWW.FACTHOUND.COM.
JUST TYPE IN THE BOOK ID: 1434215881 AND YOU'RE READY TO GO!